lessons from a dead girl

lessons from a dead girl

JO KNOWLES

CANDLEWICK PRESS
CAMBRIDGE, MASSACHUSETTS

Copyright © 2007 by Johanna Knowles

First edition 2007

Library of Congress Cataloging-in-Publication Data
Knowles, Jo, date.
Lessons from a dead girl / Jo Knowles. — 1st ed.
p. cm.
Summary: After her former friend Leah dies in an automobile accident, Laine remembers their troubled relationship, dating back to elementary school when Leah convinced Laine to "practice" in the closet with her, and Leah controlled her every thought.
ISBN 978-0-7636-3279-3
[1. Emotional problems — Fiction. 2. Sexual abuse victims — Fiction.
3. Guilt — Fiction. 4. Interpersonal relationships — Fiction. 5. Friendship — Fiction.]
I. Title.
PZ7.K7621Le 2007
[Fic] — dc22   2007025994

2 4 6 8 10 9 7 5 3 1

Printed in the United States of America

This book was typeset in Berkeley Old Style Medium.

Candlewick Press
2067 Massachusetts Avenue
Cambridge, Massachusetts 02140

visit us at www.candlewick.com

for anyone who has held a secret

after

Leah Greene is dead.

Before my mother even answers the ringing telephone downstairs, I know.

"Hello?" I hear my mother say politely. "Yes? Yes, this is Laine's mother."

There is a long, quiet pause.

"Yes? A party? Drinking? Oh . . . well—"

Another pause.

"Leah Greene? What? Oh, my God! Are you sure? How?"

As I listen to her panicked voice, I feel the tiny bricks that have walled away certain memories continue to crumble. I squeeze my eyes shut and cover my ears. But the sound of my mother's cries downstairs pushes against the wall and loosens the mortar. All I see behind my eyelids is Leah. Leah with her red-glossed lips. Leah standing above me. Leah telling our secret to a crowded room of strangers and my only friends in the world. Leah walking away, leaving me in the rubble of my ruined life.

I hate you! I wish you were dead!

I had screamed the words inside my head, as if I were seven and not seventeen. Somehow, I think she must have heard me.

Through my bedroom window, the sky is clear blue and the sun shines a warm spot on my bed, already taken by my cat, Jack. He calmly cleans his belly, his back paw bent behind his head. As he licks, I see a flash of him dressed in baby-doll clothes. Leah is holding him under his front legs and making him dance. And I see me, laughing, even though I want her to stop.

Jack closes his eyes when he finishes licking and settles his head against my foot through the covers. The fur around his eyes looks gray, and his coat is full of dandruff where he can't reach anymore.

"Good kitty," I whisper, rubbing his head through the covers with my toe. He purrs back.

My bedroom door is open. I watch it, waiting for my mother to appear.

Her steps are slow and heavy on the stairs, as if she's carrying something large inside her. She hesitates in the doorway, looking in at me safe in my bed.

"Something's happened," she says, carefully stepping into my room. Her voice is quiet. I don't move. The cat shifts and starts licking again.

My mother sits on the bed next to me and touches my shoulder. "There was an accident," she says.

I turn my head away from her.

She moves closer and tries again. "There was a"— she pauses—"a terrible accident."

She doesn't tell me what kind of accident. Maybe she doesn't want me to know the details. But it's too late for that.

Her hand presses hard against my shoulder. "Lainey?"

I should be crying or asking what happened. I should look more surprised. But all I feel is this overwhelming sense of guilt and fear, and they're fighting each other inside my chest.

It can't be true. But it is. It's over. And it's my fault.

My mother waits for me to reply, but I stay silent. I look away from her and wait for her to go.

When she finally gets up to leave, she asks if I'll be OK. I nod and roll over.

She goes back downstairs and gets on the phone again. She talks in a low, nervous voice. *Terrible accident. Terrible. Terrible.*

The thoughts in my head echo her words. *It's over. Over.*

Each time she says Leah's name, I get pulled back there, to the time when Leah and I were still best friends. The feelings come rushing into my chest. I try to shake my head. Swallow. Push them back down. Strengthen the mortar and rebuild my wall. But I see us anyway. One scene after another. Leah, always the leader, teaching me the complicated rules about trust and secrets and what it means to be her best friend. There were so many hard lessons. But what good are they now? What good are lessons from a dead girl?

LESSON 1

F. F. = Friends Forever

Leah and I are in the fifth grade. We're at recess when Leah motions me to the far side of the playground, where the boys usually play kickball, only this day it's too muddy even for them. I look around to make sure it's really me she's pointing to.

"Come on, Lainey!" she calls. Until this moment, we've only been "outside of school" friends, if you could call it that. Our sisters are friends, so they're convinced we should be, too. Every so often they try to get us to spend time together. But whenever Leah comes over or I go to her house, I can tell she wishes I was more like my sister, Christi. Or more like herself.

Christi pretends not to notice the obvious reasons Leah and I don't become close, but you would have to be blind not to see them. Leah is popular and I'm not. Leah is also beautiful. *Everyone* wants to be Leah's best friend. But me? Most people don't even know who I am. Christi doesn't get that people like Leah don't want to be friends with people like me.

"Lai-ney," Leah sings to me from across the playground. She gestures at me with her hand again.

I run to her obediently. Who wouldn't want to be seen hanging out with Leah Greene? She's smart, so the teachers love her. She's beautiful, so the boys love her. Even the boys who still say they don't like girls. And because all the boys and all the teachers love her, all the girls want to be her friend—and learn how to be just like her.

As we trudge along toward the field, our shoes sink into the mud and make a slurping sound with each step. The teacher on recess duty calls to us to stay out of the mud. Leah sings back in her sweet voice, "We wi-ill!" But we're already well into it. I keep following her until we're far enough out to be alone, even though we're in the open.

"I have a secret," she tells me, grinning. She pulls a marker in the shape of a mouse out of her jacket pocket.

The cap is the mouse's head, and when she pulls it off, there's a marker tip inside. She gives me the head to hold in one hand and takes my other hand in hers, turning it over palm up. Then I watch, amazed, as she carefully writes *L.G. + L.M. = F.F.* along the crease in my hand that she says is my lifeline. When she's done, she writes the same thing on her own palm.

"There," she says, smiling as if she's won a game. "Know what it means?"

I think I do, but I shake my head *no* anyway. *Us? F.F.?* I try not to smile too eagerly.

"Leah Greene plus Laine McCarthy equals Friends Forever," she says. Her lips part to show her white teeth as she grins at me.

My whole body smiles at her soft words. They don't make any sense, but at the moment I don't want to think about that.

Leah takes my hand again and pushes our palms together just as the bell rings. I look around to make sure no one sees us holding hands, but Leah doesn't seem to care. Her hand is warm and dry, and I feel a strange, thrilling tingle shoot right up my arm when we touch, as if she has magic inside.

Friends forever. But why?

"Don't show anyone," she says as we race side by

side to the students already lined up to go inside. Some of the girls eye us curiously.

I squeeze my hand shut and hold our secret in it. Any time I start to wonder why on earth Leah Greene wants to be my best friend, I tell myself not to think about it.

All that day, each time we see each other, we wave our closed fists and grin. I feel so deliriously happy, I think my lips will crack from smiling so hard. I sneak peeks at the purple letters on my hand to remind myself it isn't a dream. I feel taller. Better than the girls around me. I feel a difference in how I walk. How I answer Mrs. Faughnan's questions. I'm not no one anymore. I'm friends with Leah Greene. Friends forever.

LESSON 2

Forever is a long time.

F.F. with Leah Greene means I sit next to her at the popular table at lunch. It means I get invited to birthday parties. I have friends, even if they are second friends, the way you have second cousins. They're distant and it's not quite clear how you are connected, but the connection means you're invited to all the big events out of obligation, even if they don't speak to you or acknowledge that you're there.

Just before school gets out that year, Leah pulls me from our group during recess and leads me out to the field again, just like she did that first time she declared our friendship. She pulls a marker out of her coat pocket. This one is red. It's the thick kind my mom uses to make sale posters at the antique store my parents run.

Leah carefully holds my hand still while she writes F.F. on my palm. Then she writes the same on hers and presses our hands together, just like the first time. Like before, my hand tingles when she touches me. I smile when I feel it, that magic spark between us. I check her face to see if she felt something, too. She smiles back at me.

"It's permanent," she says, putting the marker in her pocket. "Like us."

We grin at each other so our teeth show. My insides dance.

Some other girls come over and plead with us to come play Leah's version of tag, which involves the girls chasing the boys until the last boy gets caught and has to pick a girl to kiss. I've never been picked. The girls smile at Leah but seem to sneer at me when she isn't looking, as if they know I hate this game and why. No boy would ever kiss me.

Last year, someone left a note on my desk that said, *Are you a boy or a girl?* I put it in my pocket and waited to reread it when I got home. Alone in my room, I carefully unfolded the note, trying to touch it as little as possible. It was written in messy pencil on yellow lined paper. I stared at the words and cried.

Christi walked in on me and made me show her the note. I tried to crumple it up in my fist, but she pried it out of my fingers.

"People are jerks," she told me. "Ignore them." Then she took the note and threw it in the woodstove.

Leah gives me her special half-smile before running away from us. Her long hair whips back and dances behind her, and we all run to keep up.

After school, my mother picks us up in our old, beat-up minivan. Leah's mom asked my mom to take Leah for the afternoon so she could bring Brooke to a doctor's appointment. Christi is at piano lessons, so when we get home, it's just Leah and me.

We race up the stairs side by side, but when we get to the top, Leah pushes past me and runs down the hall to my room. I chase after her, and we leap onto my bed so the headboard thuds against the wall.

"Let's play in the doll closet," Leah says.

The doll closet is a crouch-in closet in the upstairs bathroom that Christi and I share. It has a child-size table and chairs to sit at and a wooden play stove and refrigerator my father made for us when we were little. It also has lots of our old dolls and stuffed animals and the plastic cups and plates we used to play with for pretend tea.

"Come on," Leah says, opening the closet door and motioning for me to go in first. I click on the night-light by the door and sit at the little table.

Leah comes in after me and closes the door behind her. It's late spring, but it's cold in the closet. It smells like dust and plastic toys. The dolls seem to watch us suspiciously. Sometimes Leah and I come in here and pretend we're husband and wife and all the dolls are our babies. We make a joke out of it since we're way too old to play with dolls. Leah gets to be the wife because she has long hair and mine is short. Once we put our hands over our mouths and pressed our faces together, pretending to kiss. Leah said only real friends like us could practice like that because we would never tell anyone. It's our special secret. It makes *me* feel special to have it with her.

"Let's practice again," Leah says, as if reading my mind. She moves closer to me. "I'll be the husband this time. You're my wife, and you have to do what I say."

I start to say "OK" but Leah stops me, putting her pointer finger on my lips.

12

"Don't talk," she says. "I didn't say you could."

I stop smiling.

"Close your eyes," she whispers a little more gently.

I close them and feel her move closer to me. Her breath is warm on my face. When she puts her hands on my knees, her electricity goes right through me. I get a tingly feeling low in my stomach.

She slides her hands slowly up my thighs.

I open my eyes for a split second. Her face is so close to mine, I can see the tiny blue veins in her eyelids. My heart thumps wildly against my chest.

She puts both hands around my waist. I still don't move or dare open my eyes again.

Then she kisses me. This time, she doesn't put her hand between our lips. Her mouth pushes against mine. She moans. I'm too scared to move. But I'm excited, too. *Girls don't do this. Leah must love me. Why? What does this mean?*

A strange, prickly warmth spreads through my body. I sit perfectly still and let her kiss me. I let her hands pull me toward her until my chest presses up against hers and our hearts pound against each other. I keep my eyes closed tight and let her do what she wants.

* * *

When we step out of the closet, we don't talk. I still feel her lips on me, her chest against mine. I wonder if she feels the same way.

I follow Leah downstairs and out to the backyard, where my dog, Seal, runs up to us, holding a stick in his mouth and wagging his tail. Leah tries to take the stick from him, but he steps back and runs. We chase him, but he darts between us.

I finally get close enough to touch his tail when Leah grabs my shoulders from behind. She pulls me backward and to the ground. I land with a hard thud. Before I can get up, Leah straddles me and pins my hands to the ground. She looks down at me and makes a face like she's going to kiss me again. She looks like she wants to hurt me.

"Get off!" I say.

She laughs without opening her mouth. She pushes my wrists against the ground so hard I cry out, but she holds tighter. I try to pull my hands away, to wiggle my body out from under hers.

Then I feel it. Something warm and wet landing on my forehead. It rolls down my temple and into my ear, warm and cold at the same time.

Leah laughs out loud and climbs off me.

14

"You liked it," she says.

I roll away and sit up, quickly rubbing her spit off my face.

"I did not!" I lie, trying not to cry. I get up and run to the back door.

"You know you did!" Leah calls after me.

I don't turn around. I don't argue with her again. I know it's true. But what does it mean?

Later, after Leah's mother picks her up, I go to my room. Christi and my mom and dad are all home, but they're busy and don't notice me. I listen to their usual sounds— my sister in her room singing to a CD, my parents downstairs listening to the news and arguing with the TV. My room feels different. Leah has touched everything in here. I can even smell her.

When I turn, I see my reflection in my dresser mirror. My hair is like a boy's, short and brown and messy. My striped shirt is too small and has a grass stain on the front. Even my face is dirty. I look like a boy. An ugly boy. And I feel like one, too. Why would Leah be my friend? Why would she do those things to me? Was it all just a joke?

I grab my old Curious George and hide in my

bedroom closet, where there's only space for me. I press George's face against mine.

Why did she do it? Why did I let her? What's wrong with me?

My tears soak George's fur, but he just smiles at me in the dim light, no matter how hard I cry.

That night, when Christi and I are in the bathroom getting ready for bed, she asks me what's on my hand. I look at the slightly faded Fs.

"Nothing," I say. I scrub the letters with soap as hard as I can, but they won't come off.

"Must be permanent marker," Christi says. "Way to go, Brain."

"It will come off," I say, scrubbing harder. But even when my hand is almost raw, I still see some of the red marker.

I go back to my room and hug George again.

"We won't be friends forever," I whisper into his fur. "We won't."

But he keeps smiling, like he knows better.

The next day at school, Leah waits for me on the playground. I try to go the other way, but she chases after me.

"What's wrong?" she asks innocently.

I don't say anything. She knows the answer.

16

"Oh, Laine, it was just a silly game. You need to toughen up," she says.

"It didn't feel like a game," I tell her. I look at my feet, remembering her lips on mine, her chest pressed against mine, her spit on my face.

"OK, I'll tell you the truth," she says. "I was testing you."

"What do you mean?"

She steps closer. "You know. To see if you trusted me. We have to practice for when we get older, remember? It's what best friends do."

"Then why did you spit on me?"

"I was afraid you'd tell our secret."

"I would never!"

She sighs heavily, like she's talking to a stupid five-year-old. "You're right," she says. "I should have trusted you. I know you're not the type to break a promise. That's why we're friends."

She reaches for my hand and squeezes it, then quickly lets go before anyone sees. "Come on," she says, ending the conversation. She heads for the swings. I hesitate, wondering what she'd do if I didn't follow.

She turns back and motions to me to come with her. I don't move. She smiles, then looks around for someone else to call. I'm sure every girl in my class would die to have Leah call her name, and I panic at the thought of being replaced. I follow her.

A few weeks go by before Leah comes over again. As soon as we're alone, she takes my hand. "We need to practice," she tells me. She pulls me forward before I can answer. As her fingers lace tightly through mine, I feel her magic and let her lead me into the closet. She closes the door and we kiss. Then she rubs her hands over my body.

I'm scared and excited all over again, but I don't want her to accuse me of liking it the way she did the last time, as if something was wrong with me. So I close my eyes and try not to feel her hands on me, her lips on me, the way my stomach tightens at her touch.

We're just practicing, I tell myself. *That's all.*

LESSON 3
Winning feels good.

By the summer after sixth grade, Leah and I have had lots of practice. It's always the same. Always at my house, in front of the lifeless dolls. Leah says this is the year—when we start seventh grade, we'll start practicing with boys. Each time we go into the closet, I wonder if it will be our last, and each time we step out, I'm filled with shame over the small part of me that doesn't want it to be.

Then Mr. and Mrs. Greene decide to buy horses for Leah and Brooke, and Leah seems to forget all about the doll closet. Brooke's horse, Sunshine, is tall and a beautiful light brown. She came from a big, fancy horse farm in Massachusetts. Leah's horse, Prince, is shiny black.

Just like the Black Stallion. He also came with a pony named Lucky. Leah said the woman who owned Prince had the pony to keep Prince company and because he helped keep the horse calm. Leah threw a fit when her dad told the lady they didn't want Lucky. She cried and told him how it would be cruel to separate them. But part of me wonders if she got the pony for me.

One day when the horses and Lucky are out in the pasture, Leah takes me into one of their stalls. She stomps around and acts goofy and makes me try their grain, which is surprisingly not bad. I love when Leah and I can just be silly and act totally immature together. Leah would never do these things in front of the other girls in our group, and I like having a secret thing we do together that feels safe.

Leah is determined to teach me what she learns at her riding lessons. After each one, she forces me onto lazy Lucky's back and out to the riding ring to practice. She has her work cut out for her. The only thing Lucky wants to do is head back to the barn. But Leah does teach me how to post and get him on the right lead.

By late summer Leah and Brooke have been to several horse shows. Leah decides she wants me to go, too. She begs and begs her father to bring Lucky, even though

I say I don't want to go. Leah ignores me. She says it will be good for Lucky to get a feel for what it's like.

The day of the next show, we all get up before the sun rises and wash and braid the horses' manes. Even Lucky's. I don't know why Leah is so determined to make me a part of this horsey life. It's clear I don't fit in. Poor old Lucky and I look ridiculous next to Leah and Brooke on their fancy horses. But Leah seems blind to this. She never questions whether she can do something—and now she seems to have the same confidence in me.

At the show, I watch Leah and Brooke compete a few times, then I saddle Lucky and we walk around, checking out the expensive horse trailers. Lucky has an extra bounce in his step. I can tell he knows how pretty he looks with his mane braided and his dappled gray coat all clean and free of dust. For a little while, it feels like he's mine and that I'm a part of this world, even though my parents probably couldn't even afford to buy the saddle, much less the pony I'm riding.

Toward the end of the day, Leah comes rushing over to me. She's smiling and holding out a white paper with a number on it.

"What's that for?" I ask.

"You. We're signed up for Breaking and Out together!"

"What? I can't be in the show. I don't know how! I don't even know what Breaking and Out is!"

"It's just for fun," she tells me. "It will be perfect. You have to start somewhere, don't you?"

The next thing I know, we're walking along, looking as silly as ever. The rules are that you partner up with someone and walk your horses side by side, riding bareback, while holding a strip of newspaper. Then you have to follow the judge's instructions to walk or trot. If your strip breaks, you're out.

Prince is much taller than Lucky. I have to reach up high and Leah has to hunch down low in order for us both to keep hold of the strip. The other girls giggle at us as we enter the ring. They cover their mouths with their hands as if acting properly when they're being nasty makes it OK.

Leah holds her head high. She's dressed as if she's in an Olympic event, with her black velvet riding hat, tailored jacket, leather boots, and clean riding pants. I look pathetic next to her in my ratty T-shirt and jeans.

"We can win," she says between her teeth as we make our way down the ring. My stomach is full of knots. Lucky is extra antsy. I think he may want to run for the first time in his lazy life. Maybe for the first time, he's starting to feel like he belongs with all the special horses. I wish I felt as confident.

Leah winks when the announcer calls for us to begin trotting. Prince prances gracefully and Lucky kicks up and trots along, his little legs racing to keep up with Prince's long strides. I squeeze my knees to stay on.

I hear a few people say "Awww" as we ride by. I don't dare look anywhere but straight ahead, one hand squeezing the reins, the other holding on to the newspaper strip as if my life depends on it.

"You're doing great!" Leah calls over her shoulder. "Don't let go!"

My arm is so heavy it hurts. Poor Lucky pants and snorts like mad. I almost wish the strip would break. But I know I can't let Leah down. Lucky seems as determined as me. We're both out of place, but Leah believes in us.

"Number twelve and number seven, please exit the ring!" the announcer calls. And then, "Walk now, please walk."

Leah and I trade a smile of relief to be walking again. When I look around, I see only one other pair left!

After we walk the ring once more, the announcer calls for us to reverse directions. As we try to make a tight reverse turn, Lucky bumps Prince. Leah pulls the paper toward her. My arm goes with her, and I start sliding off.

"Hang on!" she says loudly. She narrows her eyes and grits her teeth. I don't let go.

With Prince on the inside, Lucky has to hustle around every corner to keep up. I hope Leah is the one to let go of the paper, so it won't be my fault when we lose.

"Slow down, boy," Leah keeps whispering, but Prince's ears only flick as if he's getting rid of a fly.

"Number five, please exit the ring! Number eight, congratulations! Please walk to the center."

"That's us!" Leah shouts excitedly. "You can let go now!"

I let the strip slip from my fingers and into Leah's eager grasp. She waves it over her head in big circles.

People around the ring cheer, clap, and even whistle.

One of the judges walks out with two blue ribbons and hooks them onto Lucky's and Prince's bridles. "Go ahead and do your victory lap, ladies!"

Prince leads the way, cantering. Lucky is like a little colt chasing after him. Leah keeps looking back at me, yelling, "We did it!" The crowd cheers and cheers. I'm smiling so wide, the sides of my mouth feel like they might crack.

Sitting in Mr. Greene's truck on the way home, I run my fingers over the satin ribbon with the horse-head button in the middle. When we get back to the Greenes', I start to put the ribbon in my bag so I can take it home with me. But Leah says I should hang it outside Lucky's stall so everyone can see how well he did. I still want to take it home, but I know I can't. Lucky isn't even my pony. None of this is real. Leah can try to make me fit in her horsey world all she wants, but in the end, Lucky and I will never be like Leah and Prince. Still, I'm grateful for the taste.

"You're right," I say. "Sorry."

"Don't be," she says. "You didn't know." She hangs her own ribbon on Prince's stall door.

"Are you glad you tried, Lainey? Did you like it?"

"Yes," I say.

"You could come again if you wanted. We could show together! It's no fun doing it alone." Her face looks so genuine. I want to say yes, but I know it won't work. It's one thing to be in the "just for fun" competition, but Lucky and I would never cut it in the real ones.

"Thanks," I say. "But I don't think I have what it takes."

She frowns. "You could if you really wanted to."

I shake my head. "My parents could never afford it—the clothes, the classes, the show fees . . ."

"I could get my parents to pay."

I shake my head again. "Thanks, Leah. I'm really glad for today."

She shrugs and looks away from me. I wonder if she's wishing she'd picked a friend with more money. Someone who could keep up with her. I wonder again why she picked me in the first place. But I don't ask. Today, for the first time in a long time, I just feel grateful she did.

Before I go home, I reach for the ribbon one last time and rub the soft fake satin between my fingers. I picture our victory lap around the riding ring. Leah and Prince and Lucky and me, cantering around while everyone clapped and cheered. And Leah, smiling back at me, waving that silly strip of newspaper in the air. I feel my mouth make the same wide grin it made earlier as I imagine Leah giving me her knowing look: *See how good it feels to win, Laine? Aren't you glad I showed you this?*

I wonder if what she really means is, *See what it's like to be me?* And all I can think is, *Yes. This is pretty great. And you're great for sharing it with me.*

Today, I'm really happy that Leah Greene is my friend.

LESSON 4

Never break a promise.

"Promise you won't leave me alone with Sam," Leah says.

It's the following June and seventh grade is almost over. We've climbed the ladder to the cupola, where we hang out sometimes after riding Prince and Lucky, who I'm almost too big for now. The barn is filled with fresh hay, and it smells overwhelmingly sweet.

"Why don't you want to be alone with him?" I ask.

"I just don't. Don't ask. Just promise."

"OK," I say. "I promise."

"Want to hear a scary story?" Leah pulls the small book of ghost stories she bought at the library book sale out from under a hay bale we use as a table when we have picnics up here.

"No," I say. I don't tell her, but the last time she read me a story from that book, I spent the night in my sister's room, even though I knew she'd tell me I was a baby the next morning, which she did.

"Scared?"

"No."

"I think you are." She grins that sneaky grin of hers and opens the book to a spot she's dog-eared. She clears her throat and starts to read the same story that gave me nightmares.

"Don't," I say. "I know it already. It's boring."

"You're scared."

"I just don't want to hear it again."

"Do you think it really happened?" She moves closer to me. "Do you think it's true, Lainey?"

Leah's always asking me if I think something's true or not. I think she's just trying to get me to say yes so she can tease me.

"It could be true, you know," she says quietly. "There are a lot of psychos out there."

"Yeah, but not around here," I say, squeezing my knees to my chest.

"Sure there are. What makes you think here is so special? There are crazy people everywhere. Where you least expect them. You'd be surprised."

Goose bumps poke up on my arms. She turns away from me.

A car horn and the sound of wheels crunching up the Greenes' long, stone-covered driveway save me.

Leah jumps off the dusty bale of hay she's been sitting on and stands at the window. I stand beside her and peek out to see Sam stepping from his black Jaguar.

We watch him climb out of the car and stretch. He's wearing a pair of new-looking jeans and a sports jacket. His thin, sandy hair is brushed across the top of his head.

Sam is Mr. Greene's best friend from college. He comes to visit about once a month. The Greenes think he's a god or something, though seeing him now, I have no idea why. I've never actually met him because usually I'm not invited over when he comes. But today Leah begged to let me stay.

"I better go," Leah says. She heads for the ladder without waiting for me. She's out of the barn before I reach the bottom rung.

"Wait for me!" I call. How am I supposed to not leave her alone if I can't even keep up? I watch from the doorway of the barn as Leah reaches Sam and stops a few feet away. At the same time, Brooke comes running out of the house, then Mrs. Greene steps onto the porch and waves.

Sam stands next to his Jaguar and smiles at them all. He walks closer to Leah and says something, then wraps her up in his arms. She turns her head in my direction, as if to make sure I'm coming. Sam says something to Brooke that I don't hear. She walks around in front of him, wiggling her hips.

I move toward them, conscious of my unwashed hair, grimy jeans, and dirty fingernails.

I'm not surprised when Sam doesn't notice me.

"That's my girl," he says to Brooke when she stops strutting.

"I'm fifteen, Sam. I'm not a girl anymore."

His eyes trace her body. "You'll always be my special girls," he says sweetly.

Brooke smirks at him, and he lets go of Leah to hug her.

"Who's this?" he asks when he finally notices me lurking off to the side.

"That's my best friend, Laine," Leah says, stepping between us. "Didn't Mom tell you she'd be here?"

"Right! Of course! Any friend of Leah's is a friend of mine," he says, reaching out his hand to shake. It's warm and clammy. Luckily he lets go quickly.

At dinner that night, Sam brings out gifts for Brooke and Leah. Brooke's is a bottle of perfume with a pink shell for a cap. She puts a dab behind each ear and walks around the table so everyone can sniff. I think it smells like my old great-aunts, but I pretend it smells nice.

Leah's gift is the softest sweater I've ever touched. It's pale pink with little pearl buttons. When she puts it on, her blond hair looks almost pink, too. Like Brooke, she walks around the table, letting everyone touch her sleeve. The sweater is much nicer than the little glass figurines, purses, earrings, and things Leah has shown me from Sam's other visits. I wonder what makes this visit so special.

Out of the blue, Sam steps out of the room and comes back with a gift for me, too. I can tell Leah and Brooke aren't expecting it by the way their eyes narrow. I catch them exchange a look, but I can't tell what it means.

I touch the smooth wrapping paper and turn the gift around in my hands. The ribbon is real, not like the plastic curling ribbon my mother uses. But the edges of the paper are worn and faded, as if Sam has a bunch of wrapped-up gifts lying around in case he runs into someone he needs to give a present to.

"Well, Lainey, it isn't going to unwrap itself!" Mrs. Greene says, taking another sip of her wine.

I carefully untie the ribbon. Inside the box there's an oval-shaped wooden doll, hand-painted in bright colors: red, green, yellow, blue. I touch the paint, the tiny lines that decorate the doll's body. I move my finger over the seam in the doll's middle.

"Go on, open her up!" Sam's voice booms from the end of the table.

I turn the doll's halves and sure enough they come apart, revealing another doll inside, with a similar seam in the middle. When I open that doll, there's another.

Sam chuckles as I open the dolls. "I hope you like dolls, Lainey!"

Not since the second grade, I don't say. Instead I nod politely as I open them, leaving the doll shells lined up neatly on my linen place mat. The dolls get smaller and smaller until, just when I think there can't possibly be a smaller one, I find a tiny doll without a seam. She's painted all red, except for her face, and she's solid.

Mrs. Greene repeats about a thousand times how generous Sam is while we eat dessert. She's had quite a few refills of wine, and so have Sam and Mr. Greene. Leah and Brooke beg for sips and get a few, but I don't ask and no one offers.

After dessert, Mrs. Greene ushers everyone into the living room, which is not to be mistaken for the family room. The living room is off-limits except for special company, like Sam. I've never even sat on the couch before. The glass French doors to the room are always firmly closed whenever I'm there.

Mr. Greene winds up the old Victrola he bought from my parents' antique store. The scratchy music that comes out sounds like an old movie.

I sit cross-legged on the floor, not sure what to do with my new doll. When I shake it, the smaller dolls rattle inside.

Mr. and Mrs. Greene sit on the light-blue velvet couch that looks like it's never been sat on. Leah and Brooke sit on either side of them, their hands on the armrests. Sam's already doing some sort of two-step around the shiny living-room floor. Slowly, he sashays his way onto the Oriental rug in front of the couch. He holds out his hands to Brooke and Leah. Brooke jumps up and starts dancing with him, but Leah stays put. Sam reaches for her hand and pulls her toward him, smiling and looking into her eyes. She stands reluctantly. He pulls her gently to the middle of the room. When Brooke steps in to join them, Leah starts to move to the music.

Sam holds their hands and makes them twirl in synchronized circles. The longer they dance, the more Leah seems to enjoy it. They all do.

Mr. and Mrs. Greene watch, smiling, as Sam tries to dance like he's in high school. I actually feel embarrassed for him. His forehead is wet, and the hair he brushes over the top of his head keeps slipping down so he has to flip it back over. I seem to be the only one to notice.

I hold the doll over the polished floor and make her dance above it so I don't have to watch Sam and "his girls." I set the doll down and try to spin her, but she just wobbles in an awkward circle and tips over. When I pick her up, there's a small scratch in the floor. I quickly lick my finger and try to wipe the scratch out, but it doesn't go away. I check to see if the Greenes noticed, but they're too busy dancing and singing to each other.

I decide I need to go to the bathroom.

No one notices me leave. Instead of going back to the party, I go to Leah's room and climb into my sleeping bag on the floor. I lie there and wait while the music goes on and on. I try not to think of sweaty Sam dancing with Leah and Brooke. Pretty soon it gets quiet, and I hear Mr. and Mrs. Greene giggling off to their bedroom. But there's no sign of Leah.

I don't know what time it is when Leah finally comes into the room. I must have drifted off. Leah doesn't notice that I'm awake. She pads across the room to her dresser. She rummages through the drawer for a long time. I try to see what she's doing, but it's too dark. She keeps sniffling. At first I think she has a runny nose, but then I realize she's crying.

It's the first time I've ever heard her cry.

I don't dare move. I'm sure she wouldn't want me to know.

When she finally gets what she's looking for, she closes the drawer. She starts to walk toward the bed and stops near my feet. I keep my eyes closed and breathe steadily so she'll think I'm asleep.

She sniffs and makes a sound like she's wiping her eyes or nose with her hand. Then, instead of getting undressed, she crawls into bed. I hear her moving around in the bed above me. After a while, she throws something down on the floor next to me. I slowly reach my hand out and touch her soft pink sweater.

It's quiet now, except for her steady sniffling. I should say something, but I don't know what.

Promise you won't leave me alone with Sam, she'd said.

But I didn't. She was with her family, having a good time. She was with Sam, but she wasn't alone.

So why do I feel guilty?

In the morning, Sam offers to take me home in his Jaguar. Leah and Brooke insist on coming along. Leah and I sit in the tiny backseat. She pretends to be a movie star, waving out the window to invisible fans. Only Leah could do that without being embarrassed.

"You really could be a star, honey," Sam says. He smiles at her in the rearview mirror.

Leah doesn't answer him.

When we turn onto my road, Leah looks over at the wooden doll in my hands. "Let me borrow it for a while," she says. She reaches over and takes the doll from me. I think I see Sam give her a fake disapproving look, but I can't be sure.

As soon as they drop me off, I go to my room and shut the door. My old Curious George smiles disapprovingly at me from the shelf. "What did I do?" I ask.

But I know. Leah took the doll because I let her down. I broke my promise and Sam did something to her. I don't know what specifically, but I know it wasn't good.

*   *   *

The following weekend, Leah comes to my house. She pulls me straight into the doll closet. She doesn't ask or even tell me what we're going to do. She's rough and angry. It doesn't feel like practice. It feels like punishment.

I hold myself as stiff as I can, my eyes squeezed shut, feeling like I deserve it.

LESSON 5

Secrets can be used against you.

"Sam says we could be supermodel sisters," Leah says, sticking out her chest.

It's the fall of eighth grade. Leah and Brooke are strutting down the catwalk that is the path between the twin beds in Christi's room. They have light blue bath towels wrapped around their heads like turbans. They swing their hips as they walk, pretending to pose for photographers.

Christi and I watch from Christi's bed with our mouths open.

"Sam says they make *tons* of money," Leah adds.

Christi and I had watched Sam from Christi's window when he dropped Leah and Brooke off here earlier.

He kissed them both good-bye on the lips. I swear his hand brushed against Leah's butt as she walked away from him. If it did, she didn't seem to respond. The way she talks about him now, you'd never know he was the same guy she didn't want to be left alone with.

"And if it doesn't work out, we could always be strippers," Brooke says, lifting up her shirt to just below her breasts. She and Christi are sophomores, but Brooke looks more like a college girl. Brooke is beautiful, like Leah. But that's their only similarity. Brooke doesn't have the same "I'm in charge" look in her eyes. She just seems to like being watched.

"How pathetic," Christi says, nudging me with her elbow.

Brooke stands above us and sticks out her chest. She turns, a graceful little half-step, her hands on her hips. "If you've got it, flaunt it. That's what my mother says."

Christi jabs me in the ribs again, and we exchange knowing looks. Mrs. Greene is always wearing low-cut blouses that show the tops of her large breasts.

"Flaunt it? That's so—slutty," Christi says, wrinkling her nose.

"What's slutty about it?" Leah asks. "Just because you show off your goods doesn't mean you're giving them away." She's gathered the waist of her T-shirt and pulled it through the neck, making a halter top out of it. She walks up to us and sticks her bare stomach close to our faces. Her eye-like belly button watches me.

"Don't be gross," Christi says.

But Leah keeps her stomach inches from my face.

I feel my own stomach tighten the way it does when Leah and I are in the doll closet. My cheeks go prickly hot.

"What do you think, E-laine? Am I gross?" she asks.

I don't answer.

"Don't call her that. You know she hates it." Christi moves closer to me on the bed, going into protector mode.

Leah ignores her. "E-laine, *you* don't think I'm gross, *do* you?"

"Leave her alone," Christi says. She sounds nervous, as if she knows what Leah is getting at.

I force myself to look up into Leah's face and plead with my eyes for her not to say anything. Leah smirks and turns around.

Later that afternoon, Christi and Brooke are outside practicing new cheers for tryouts. Leah and I are alone in my room.

"Let's play house," Leah says quietly. "We haven't practiced in a while."

"I don't think so," I say, remembering what it was like the last time.

She moves closer. "Please, Lainey. It will be fun," she says softly. She looks almost sad, like I hurt her feelings by not wanting to go. She reaches for my hand and tries to pull me. Her hand feels delicate and strong at the same time.

"I don't want to," I say. As she laces her fingers with mine, though, I feel that strange, familiar tingling in my stomach. I shake my head, but even as I do, I'm already walking with her up the stairs.

Once we're inside the closet, Leah shuts the door. I turn on the tiny light. Leah comes closer, raising her eyebrows.

I close my eyes and pretend I'm someone else. I pretend I'm one of the dolls, sitting in the corner, watching Leah kiss me and put her hands up my shirt and down my pants, feeling every part of me, then taking my hands and making me feel every part of her. I try not to let it feel good, but it does. It feels good and horrible at the same time. Every part of my body feels alive.

"Right here," she says.

"Right there," she whispers.

Her voice is deep and not like her own. It scares me. Why is it that the only times I feel really alive are when I'm terrified?

When it's over and Leah opens the door, Christi is standing there, looking at us.

"What were you guys doing in there?" she asks. Her face is pale.

I feel like I'm going to throw up.

I pray Christi won't look in my eyes, because if she does, I'm sure she'll know. I hear her words from earlier. *Don't be gross.*

But I know what she really meant, because it's how I feel now. *Dirty.*

Leah clears her throat. "Playing house," she says coolly. She walks past Christi as if that's all she needs to say.

I stay put, looking at the floor. Eighth-graders don't play house.

I wait for Christi to say so, but she just turns and leaves, careful to avoid making eye contact with me.

Later, when Leah and I are alone outside, I tell her I'm finished with practicing.

Leah shrugs her shoulders. "I don't care," she says casually.

I feel my mouth drop open. *Then why do you make me do it?!* I want to scream. She makes her own mouth drop open to imitate me. Then she turns and walks away. I swear I see her smile, as if she's had a new idea.

"I was just talking to Zack Wallace," she tells me the next week at school. "I was telling him about this neat closet you have in your house. How you call it the doll closet, and how we used to play in it together." She smiles, showing me her white teeth. One of her top front teeth crosses over the other just slightly. It's one of Leah's only flaws, and I always catch myself looking at it when she talks to me.

"Leah, please," I say. "You can't tell anyone."

She grins at me. "Why not?"

"Because—" But I don't know how to answer. And, anyway, she knows.

"You said it was a secret," I tell her.

"A secret is like a promise," she says. "And you broke a promise to me. Maybe if I tell the secret, we'll be even."

"But I didn't—" I want to tell her I didn't mean to break the promise about Sam. But the more I think about it, the more I'm not sure.

We look at each other, both waiting for the other to say something. The words I want to ask are in the back of my throat. *What happened with Sam? What did he do?* But when I open my mouth to force them out, Leah rolls her eyes at me and walks away.

LESSON 6

All closets hold secrets.

"Let's see if your dad has any dirty magazines," Leah says. She's found my old Barbie suitcase in my closet and is making Ken and Malibu Barbie do obscene things to each other.

"Why do you keep these things, anyway? My mom gave away all my old toys." She digs through the suitcase and finds Skipper. "Looks like you, Lainey!" She laughs, pointing at my chest.

I roll my eyes.

"You still play with them, don't you?"

I'm used to this. Ever since I broke my promise, Leah has gotten increasingly nasty.

"I don't play with them," I say. "My dad says they'll be worth a lot some day."

I grab the dolls and shove them back in their case. "And my dad does *not* have dirty magazines," I add. "He's not like that."

"Like what? There's nothing wrong with looking. That's what my dad tells my mom."

"Well, my dad doesn't," I tell her.

"Whatever." Leah smiles. "But I bet he does."

"How would you know?" There is no way my father looks at that stuff. "The only time my dad ever had a *Playboy* is the one he got at the surprise party my mom had for him when he turned forty."

"*Mmm-hmm,*" Leah says. I want to hit her. She reaches over and puts her hand on my thigh. "Prove it."

My cheeks get hot with her touch, and a familiar, horrible warm feeling fills my stomach—and lower down. I feel my body wake up with excitement and the fear that always comes with it.

"I told you my dad doesn't have any. He's not like that."

"We'll see." Leah stands and walks out of my room.

As the stairs creak under her weight, I know I'm going to follow. I don't want her looking through my parents' stuff without me. I look out the window to make sure my mom is still outside in the garden, then I follow.

I hear Leah in my parents' bedroom. When I go in, I find her searching through my father's closet.

"Hey! What are you doing?"

"Looking," she says, all serious. She pushes her way farther into the back of the closet. Sure enough, behind a small pile of shoes he never wears, Leah hits the jackpot. A cardboard wine box, ripped on one side, is hidden behind a white plastic bag that has *summer clothes* written on it in Magic Marker.

Leah pulls open the flaps and snickers.

"I told you," she said, holding up a *Playboy* magazine. There's a blond woman with huge breasts and a toothy smile on the cover. "My mom says *all* men keep their *Playboy*s in the closet. So predictable." She says the last bit in her know-it-all voice. I still can't believe it, but there it is. In her hands.

Leah shoves the magazine under her shirt. "Come on!" She pushes past me and makes her way back up to my bedroom.

I stay behind and push the plastic bag back against the cardboard box deep in the closet. The closet smells like my father, only it's a stale him, mixed with must and old wool. I quickly step back out into the room.

48

It feels different in here—the sweet blue flowers on the wallpaper, the silver frame with my parents' wedding picture, Christi's and my tiny plaster handprints hanging from pink ribbons—it all feels fake. I shut my father's closet door. How could something so nasty exist in this room?

"E-laine!" Leah calls in a singsong voice from upstairs.

It's wrong. I know it. But I go to her anyway. She's lying on her stomach on my bed. She looks up and smiles when she sees me, then pats the space beside her.

I join her. She has the magazine opened to a picture of a woman with red hair sitting in a chair with her legs spread open. She's smiling.

Leah turns the pages while we both stare, speechless. My body tingles all over. I feel the same fear and excitement I felt in the doll closet. I hate it. But I keep looking.

Suddenly we hear the back door open downstairs and my mother's footsteps wandering through the house.

"Girls?" she calls out.

"Hide it!" I whisper loudly.

Leah laughs. "You should see your face," she says.

"Leah, please," I plead. "Put it under the mattress."

She stands up with the magazine in her hands.

"What's wrong, Laine? Afraid your mother will catch us?"

"Yes!"

Leah rolls her eyes. "It's only a stupid magazine. What's the big deal?"

"Girls?" my mother calls from downstairs. "Are you ready for some lunch?" I hear her feet starting up the stairs. I know at that moment something awful is going to happen.

"Hide it. Please," I whisper.

Leah dances around the bedroom, swirling the magazine above her head. The blond woman on the cover smiles at me, her large white breasts laughing.

I lunge for the magazine, pull it out of Leah's hands, and manage to shove it under the mattress right as my mother reaches the top of the stairs.

Leah seems surprised, but only for a second. She giggles.

"What are you girls doing?" my mother asks from the doorway.

"Nothing," I say.

"Well, not *nothing*, Laine," Leah says.

God, I want to kill her. My heart beats so hard and fast it hurts. Sweat prickles out all over my body, hot and cold at the same time.

50

"We were playing, right, Lainey?" Leah giggles again and sits on the bed.

"What are you up to?" my mother asks suspiciously.

"Nothing," I say again. But she's already caught on.

"Why is the dust ruffle on your bed tucked into the mattress?"

I look. The edge of the magazine is sticking slightly out from under the mattress. I'd shoved it under so quickly, I pushed the dust ruffle in, too.

"What is that?"

"Nothing," I answer quickly.

Leah giggles again.

My mother pulls the magazine out from under the mattress and looks at the cover. Her mouth drops open. She rolls the magazine to hide the cover. Leah keeps giggling. But she sounds nervous now.

"Where did you get this?"

I don't answer. Leah can't stop making those awful giggle sounds.

"Where?!"

Leah laughs out loud. I glare at her. "Shut up!" I scream.

My mother grabs my arm so hard, her fingers dig into my muscle.

I pull away and run out of the room, down the

stairs, and outside. Out to the pathway in the woods that leads to the big rock Leah and I used to hang out on when we first became friends. We pretended it was an island and we were stranded on it and had to come up with ways we could survive.

I climb the rock and sit on top of it, hugging my knees to my chest. Through the woods and my tears, I see our white farmhouse. It looks quiet, but I know it isn't. I watch, waiting for some sign of my mother. Or Leah.

I've never felt this ugly or embarrassed—this dirty—in my life. I hate the way I feel. I hate it. I'm a pervert. Why else would my body feel that way when I looked at those pictures?

I will never be able to face my mother again.

After a while, I hear leaves crunching in the distance. It's Leah. She climbs the rock and sits next to me.

I move a little bit away. "What do you want?" I say without looking at her.

"She found the rest," Leah says. She doesn't tell me she's the one who told my mother where to look, but I'm sure she did. She doesn't say she's sorry.

Leah and I sit on the rock and watch the house in silence. Waiting.

Soon the back door opens, and my mother marches to the outdoor grill pit with the cardboard box in her arms. She throws it in the pit and runs back into the house. A few minutes later, she returns with a bottle of something in her hand. It must be lighter fluid. She squirts liquid all over the box, then lights the match. The whole thing goes up in flames.

I watch my mother through the smoke. She steps back and turns away from the heavy grayness, walks back to the house, and disappears inside.

The smell of the burnt magazines reaches our rock.

"Men," Leah says, shaking her head and wrinkling her nose at the smell.

I turn and watch her look at the scene she's created. Her eyes are slightly squinted so she has tiny wrinkles at the corners of her eyes. It's like looking at an adult almost, the way those wrinkles map out across her temples.

She catches me watching her, but she doesn't say anything. She just keeps shaking her head and looking at the burning magazines. I swear she's trying not to smile. But then she says without looking at me, "I didn't think that would happen, you know."

I'm not sure what part she means—finding the

magazines, getting caught, telling my mother where they were, or the way they made me feel.

"You shouldn't have done it," I say.

"I know. I'm sorry." She shifts a little next to me. "Your mom shouldn't make you feel bad about looking. There's nothing wrong with it. Besides, I'm sure it's not you she's really upset with. It's your dad."

I smell the smoke again and hope she's right. I want to ask her if she felt the way I did when she looked at the pictures, but I don't dare. I couldn't bear to be the only one.

We stay there for a long time, not saying anything. Just watching the smoke rise into the sky and disappear.

My mom never says a word to me about the magazines. But a few weeks later, my parents have a bunch of friends over for dinner. They're all sitting at the long harvest table my parents use in the dining room. Leah's spending the night, and we're spying on them from the top of the stairs. It's late, and dinner has been over for a while. They're drinking and laughing and sharing old stories about all the so-called crazy things they did when they were younger.

When he was fifteen, Mr. Murphy stole his dad's

truck and took it to the drive-in and got caught making out with his girlfriend. Mrs. Carey almost got kicked out of college for smoking pot in her dorm room. "I only hope my own kids don't put me through what I put my parents through." She laughs.

"Amen to that," my dad says.

Then my mother, who rarely speaks at these gatherings, suddenly pipes up. I can tell she's been drinking because her voice is louder than usual and a little slurred.

"Lainey and Leah certainly got started recently," she says.

Leah grabs my arm, and we exchange surprised looks. We lean closer to the top stair so we can hear better.

"Did I tell you what I caught them with?"

"Uh-oh," says Mr. Murphy. "They didn't get into your Scotch, did they, Stan?"

My dad chuckles nervously. "Honey, I don't think Laine would be thrilled to have you tell this story."

"Or out *him*," Leah whispers. I put my finger to my lips to shut her up.

"Oh, she doesn't care," my mom says, like it's no big deal.

I wish I could dash down the stairs and scream at my mom to shut up before it's too late. But I want to stay invisible, too. I don't want to exist.

"Lainey and Leah found Stan's *Playboy*s and had one up in Lainey's room," my mom says, as if she's telling one of a hundred innocent family stories. "I couldn't believe it! I guess they're at that *curious* stage." She laughs. *Everyone* laughs.

My cheeks burn. Leah shakes her head.

"Poor girls," my mom continues. "I guess I over-reacted a little."

"A little?" my dad says. "She burned all my magazines!"

They laugh again.

"My boys got into mine last year," Mr. Sloane says.

"Ha!" Leah whispers in my ear. "Those Sloanes are cute. Now we've got the goods on them."

"Yeah, but it's *normal* for boys to look at that stuff," I whisper back.

"It's normal for girls, too. God, Laine." She inches closer to the top of the stairs to hear more.

"Kids are curious," says Mrs. Carey. "When our Sarah is older, I'm going to buy her *The Joy of Sex* and tell her everything she wants to know."

"Well, after what Laine and Leah saw, I'm going to

have to ask *them*," my mother jokes. "*I* didn't even know Stan had those magazines," she whines.

I am never speaking to her again, I vow. I slide back into the hallway and tiptoe to my room. Leah follows and shuts the door behind her.

I sit on the bed and squeeze my pillow.

"You know why she told, don't you?" Leah asks, sitting next to me.

I shake my head.

"She wants them to tell her it's OK. That we're normal. And I bet she wants to get back at your dad, too."

I throw myself backward on the bed and hide my face in my pillow. "I bet they all think we're perverted," I say into my pillowcase.

"Oh, Laine," Leah says, as if she's my big sister. "Lighten up. You're reading way too much into this. Here's the deal: your mom only told so she could get back at your dad and *maybe* because she was a little worried about us. But now her friends are all going to convince her we're just 'curious,' so she'll feel better."

I roll over to face Leah. She has the strangest way of knowing things—hidden things—about people. Most of the time it scares me, because it's usually me she's seeing through.

"That's all we are, right?" I ask. "Curious?"

"Of course," she says. She grabs my old Curious George from the bookcase and sits him on her lap like a baby. "Everyone does it. My mom even showed me and Brooke my dad's stash. She told us any time we were curious, we could look. How else are you going to learn? They don't teach it at school. They don't teach us anything we really need to know. They don't teach us crap."

"But did they—you know—make you feel funny?"

She gives me a strange look, and I immediately wish I'd kept quiet. I just let her in on a secret I don't understand and that I'm afraid of. I wait for her to decide what she's going to do with it.

But in the end she simply shrugs. "That's normal, too, Lainey. Don't worry about it."

She tosses George on the bed as she gets up and walks over to my mirror. "I keep telling you, Lainey. You need to lighten up. You take everything way too seriously. All the wrong things, anyway."

She pulls her hair back with her hands, piling it on top of her head, then looks at herself from side to side to study her profile. "There's a lot more serious stuff to worry about," she says, still looking at herself. "Trust me."

LESSON 7

Everyone has something to hide.

At the end of the school year, Leah sends out invitations to a swimming and slumber party for her closest friends. It's early June, and the water is sure to be freezing. But Leah says anyone who won't go in the water is a wimp, so none of us complain.

We meet at her house on Saturday afternoon. The Greenes' house is on a small private lake that can only be used by residents who live on the road that surrounds it. There's a beach house and a raft you can swim to.

None of the girls act surprised when Paige Larson gets dropped off in a rusty Ford pickup, even though we're all in shock, which I'm sure is exactly what Leah was going for.

I don't like it. I have a bad feeling.

Paige Larson isn't popular. She's hardly even known, except to be made fun of for coming to school wearing the same thing almost every day. Or smelling like stale cigarettes and sweat.

Paige Larson doesn't say much. I think she tries to stay invisible. She hasn't lived here that long, and no one knows where she came from. I don't think anyone has ever asked.

Not long after she moved here, Paige and Charlie Briggs were paired up as lab partners in science. Charlie is another kid no one really likes for the same reasons they don't like Paige. He smells and he's poor. I hate to admit that those are the reasons, but I know it's true. Paige laughed because Charlie dropped the earthworm they were dissecting and he screamed. When she opened her mouth, her lips stretched out across her brown and yellow teeth. She quickly covered her hand with her mouth, but it was too late.

"Look at Paige's teeth!" Charlie squawked—probably because he wanted to divert attention from his own embarrassing scream.

Everyone started urging her to open her mouth.

"Come on, Paige—show us!" they taunted. Paige looked like she was going to cry. She pushed back her stool at the lab table and took off for the bathroom.

Ever since that day, Paige only smiles with her mouth closed.

She smiles that way now as she says good-bye to her mother.

"Be good," her mother says in a gruff voice. Paige nods and watches her mother drive away. She looks scared. I don't blame her.

"Hey, Paige," Leah says, almost skipping over to her. "Ready for some fun?"

I catch the other girls exchanging looks. I'm sure, like me, they're wondering what the joke is.

"Let's go, girls!" Mr. Greene calls from his giant SUV. We climb in with our towels and flip-flops, nudging each other and giggling.

At the beach, Leah parades around in her new white terry-cloth robe that her mother gave her for an early birthday present. All the girls carefully take off their clothes and pull self-consciously at their new bathing suits. I frown at the thought of revealing my faded hand-me-down suit that Christi wore two summers ago.

Paige stands off to the side, smoothing the sand with her toes.

Leah notices her the same time I do. "What's wrong, Paige? Didn't you bring a suit?" she asks.

They stare at each other. Paige seems to say something, even though no words come out. Leah nods, then turns to her mother.

"Doesn't the beach house have extra suits?" she asks.

"Of course," says Mrs. Greene, almost too sweetly. "Come with me, Paige. I'm sure we can find something that will do."

The other girls look curious, but they don't ask Leah why she invited Paige to the party. It's clear Leah has chosen Paige to be in our group, and none of us are going to risk Leah's disapproval by making some snide comment.

That's when it occurs to me that when I first became friends with Leah, I wasn't all that different from Paige. I didn't have any friends. I was quiet. Unpopular. We weren't as poor as Paige seems to be, but we obviously didn't have anywhere near what the Greenes did. Back then, no one seemed to like me any more than they like Paige now.

Is Leah planning to replace me?

We stand around quietly, as if the party has to go on hold until Paige returns.

She comes back a few minutes later, following Mrs.

Greene. She's holding a clubhouse towel tightly around herself.

Comfortable to continue the party now that Paige is back, the other girls start shouting, "Let's go! Last one in is a rotten egg!" as if we're in the first grade.

But Leah, Paige, and I just stand there. I wait for Leah to go first, knowing full well that if I go anywhere near the water before Leah, I'll get splashed.

Paige stands awkwardly behind us.

"Does the suit fit OK?" Leah asks.

I've never seen Leah show so much concern for someone before. I don't even recognize her tone of voice.

"Come on—it can't be that bad," she says gently, reaching for Paige's towel.

Paige looks pale. More than that, she looks scared.

"I'll show you mine if you show me yours," Leah says lightly. Before Paige can answer, Leah pulls off her new robe and hands it to me.

"Come on," Leah says again. "Trust me."

Paige clutches the towel tightly to her body, then takes a deep breath. Her bottom lip quivers as she slowly lets Leah take the towel from her.

Leah gasps, and yet she doesn't seem surprised by what she sees. She shakes her head.

I don't say a word. I don't move a muscle. I stand there, frozen, still clutching Leah's soft robe.

Paige's body is covered with bruises. Most of them are on her upper arms and shoulders. I swear I can make out the shape of the hand that made them. Yellow and deep purple, it's clear they're all in different stages of healing. That as soon as one started to disappear, another took its place.

Leah quickly tears her robe from my hands and gives it to Paige.

"Here, put this on," she says.

Paige does. She looks at the ground.

The other girls squeal and splash in the distance. Mr. Greene kicks water at them from the shoreline, and Mrs. Greene jokingly hollers at him to stop.

We stand absolutely still, not looking at each other.

Leah puts her shorts back on. "I'm too cold to go swimming, anyway. I'm not in the mood."

"Me, neither," I say.

Paige gathers her things and goes back inside the clubhouse to dress in private.

Leah paces while Paige is gone, biting her lower lip.

"Leah," I say, "we have to tell."

She stops pacing and looks me in the eye. "No. I told her she could trust me."

"But that was before she took the towel off. You mean you already *knew*?"

The door of the clubhouse opens, and Paige steps out.

"How did you know?" I whisper.

But Leah turns away from me and waves Paige over.

Paige returns, holding the suit, which Leah tosses through the open window of her dad's truck. Then the three of us go down to the shoreline and join Mr. Greene, kicking water at the other girls.

Later, Leah, Paige, and I sit under a tree and make designs in the sand with our fingers.

When Paige leaves briefly to use the bathroom, I try again. "We have to tell," I whisper. "Someone is *hurting* her."

"No," Leah says. She shakes her head and digs her heels into the sand. Her feet are already slightly tan, making her heels look whitish pink. Even her toes are graceful.

"But someone should know," I say. "We have to do something."

"We can't," she says.

"Why not?"

"Everyone has secrets. They aren't ours to tell.

Besides, telling could make it even worse for her. We can't risk it. All we can do is be her friends." She rubs out the lines in the sand she made with her foot. "Be glad you don't have secrets like hers."

I notice she said "you" and not "we." I immediately think of Sam, but Leah's expression tells me not to go there.

"But if we know someone's being hurt, we should tell!" I say, thinking about both Paige and Leah. "Who cares about stupid secrets!"

"No." She gives me one of her piercing looks.

I squirm, digging my own heels into the sand.

When Paige comes back, none of us say anything. I give Leah one last pleading look. She glares a silent *no* back at me.

I get up and leave the two of them sitting there.

When we get back to the house, Leah acts especially cheerful, urging everyone to have a second piece of birthday cake. She makes sure Paige has a seat next to her. Later we climb into our sleeping bags spread out on Leah's bedroom floor. Leah puts Paige's sleeping bag next to hers before I can spread mine there. *This is it,* I think. *Paige is the new me.* Maybe I should be relieved.

Leah reads scary stories from that same stupid book, even though she knows them all by heart. That thing is like a bible to her. The other girls listen closely, but all I do is watch Leah and Paige sitting in their sleeping bags as if they're best friends. Best friends with a secret.

After the other girls fall asleep, I lie awake listening to them breathe around me. I wonder if Paige is awake, too, safely next to Leah and away from whoever it is that gives her those bruises. I pick my head up and look over at her sleeping peacefully in the soft moonlight coming through the window. Then I see Leah. Her eyes are open, watching the ceiling.

I quickly put my head back down, hoping she didn't see me.

I wonder if she's worrying about Paige's secret, too. I wonder how she seemed to know about it before she saw the bruises.

I think about that night with Sam. How Leah stayed awake crying. How I should have asked if she was OK. How I was too afraid to learn the truth.

A week later, the yearbook comes out. All the graduating eighth-graders had to submit a favorite quote or poem or something to go next to their photos.

It doesn't take long for everyone to find Paige's letter to the class on page 32, just under the photo of her sad, closed-mouthed face.

To all the eighth-graders but one,

I won't see any of you again because I am moving
to Texas. You will never have to look at me again. I
am glad I won't have to go to the same school as
you from now on. Leah Greene is the only nice
person in this school.

—Paige Larson

I expect Leah to gloat when she reads Paige's note, but she doesn't. She closes the yearbook and stares at the cover. Even though the teachers who decided to print that letter now have Leah on an even higher pedestal than they already did, Leah seems sadder to me. I'll never know if she was going to replace me with Paige or if she was only trying to be nice to a girl who needed a friend.

I think about Paige and her mother driving all the way to Texas in their rusting-out pickup. How they'll be all squished together with their things. I wonder if it's Paige's mother who beats her, or someone else. Maybe her father. Or her mother's boyfriend.

I realize I don't really know anything about Paige. I don't know if she lives with both of her parents or only her mother. She seemed to suddenly come into our lives and then, just as quickly, leave.

I feel afraid for her. I want to find her and ask how I can help. I want to force her to tell someone what's happening to her. I want to tell someone myself. But I'm afraid. Especially now, when it seems way too late.

I reread Paige's letter quite a few times that summer. Every time I read it, I feel sadder. Part of me feels a little betrayed. After all, I was there, too. I saw the bruises just as Leah did. I kept her secret, too. Why didn't she put my name on that letter?

But I know why. Leah went out of her way to invite Paige to the party. I don't want to admit it, but I know I never would have done that. Leah made sure we kept the bruises a secret. And I know I wouldn't have done that, either.

We never see Paige again. Leah writes to her once, but the letter comes back, saying there's no such address. Leah frowns when she shows it to me. She pulls out a tiny scrap of paper Paige had left in her locker.

"I don't get it," she says. "I wrote the address exactly the way it is here."

"Maybe they decided to go someplace else." *Or maybe they're in hiding,* I think. I hope wherever she is, she's away from the bruise-maker. No thanks to Leah or me.

It's midsummer and hot, and we're sitting in Leah's

bedroom waiting for Mrs. Greene to put her swimsuit on so we can go down to the lake.

"I guess we'll never know," Leah says quietly, as if she's going to cry.

I start to move my hand toward her shoulder. I mean to place it there softly, just to let her know—I'm not sure what. That I'm here. That I understand. But as my hand is about to touch her, Leah takes it. She squeezes it so hard it hurts, but I don't pull away.

It's been a long time since the doll closet, but now it's as if we're back there again. Leah taking my hand.

You're my wife.

My stomach goes all funny again. But it quickly moves into the back of my throat, and I feel like I'm going to throw up.

Leah lets go of my hand. "I'm sorry," she says. Then she stands and leaves me there by myself.

I stay where I am, staring at the white spots on my hand until they slowly regain their color and fade away.

I know at this moment that I will never understand Leah Greene. Maybe no one will. But I also know that Leah isn't the strong, untouchable person I always thought she was. I've seen her weak side twice now, and I know that when Leah feels pain, it goes deep into her soul.

70

LESSON 8

When in doubt, apply the friendship test.

The following fall, Leah and I get Mr. Mitchell for fresh-man English. He is surprisingly beautiful, and all the girls love him. Even Leah acts somewhat goofy in front of him.

He says stuff other teachers don't. He writes swear words on the board and makes us stare at them until they become meaningless. He tells us stories that make us think. He asks us questions and actually seems to want to hear the answers. *Our* answers. Not his.

One day, we're sitting in class, and he asks us what a true friend is. We all raise our hands, but he motions for us to put them down. "I'll tell you," he says seriously.

"I have this friend, Jake," Mr. Mitchell says, sitting on the edge of his desk. "One day, I needed a favor. It wasn't a big favor, but I called him and told him I needed something. Know what he said?"

We shake our heads.

"He said, 'Sure.' Before he even knew what I was going to ask him. You know why?"

We shake our heads again.

"Because he trusted me not to ask him to do something he couldn't or wouldn't want to do. He knew that whatever I asked for, he would help me simply because he was my friend and I needed help. That's true friendship."

I'm sitting in the second row, staring at his faded jeans and slightly wrinkled white oxford shirt. The top two buttons are undone to show his tan chest. His hair is messy in a nice sort of way. His olive green eyes smile at us. He really is beautiful.

"Do you get it?" he asks us. We all nod silently.

Toward the end of class, Leah passes me a note. I open it carefully.

Lainey, I need to ask you a favor.

There's a smiley face at the bottom, with one eye a line instead of a dot, to show a wink. I grin and write *Sure* with another winking smiley face. Then I fold up the note, wait for Mr. Mitchell to turn around, and toss it

72

on the floor near Leah's foot so she can cover it with her shoe and pick it up.

Leah sits behind and diagonal to me. I hear the paper rustle as she unfolds it, and then the brief quiet as she looks at my response. Somehow I know she's smiling, and I can't help feel that I've passed a test. Until I start to wonder what she'll ask me to do.

As I sit there feeling anxious, I think of Mr. Mitchell's definition. If Leah's a true friend, she can't ask me to do anything I wouldn't want to. That makes me feel better. Slightly. But *is* she a true friend? There are lots of things Leah has made me do that I didn't think I wanted to. But somehow, in the end, I always let them happen without a fight.

It isn't long before the friendship test becomes a big joke with the boys. You can't go to lunch or walk down the halls without hearing someone say, "Would you do me a favor?" Leah says they're just jealous because the girls love Mr. Mitchell. She says she and I are the only ones who really understand what Mr. Mitchell was getting at.

The funny thing is Leah never does ask me for that favor.

*   *   *

About a week after the friendship lesson, we're in Mr. Mitchell's class again and Tyler Michelson is complaining about some homework assignment. "I hate algebra," he says. "Mrs. Gray gives out way too much homework."

A few other students start in on Mrs. Gray and how unfair she is and how she never explains anything.

Mr. Mitchell tells us to quiet down. "We only hate what we don't understand," he says matter-of-factly.

That shuts us all up. A bunch of people start nodding as they seem to go through their secret "I hate" lists and realize he's right.

Leah smiles at me, not knowing—or maybe I just don't think so at the time—what I just thought when I saw her face: *She has been on my list.*

She pats her heart, our sign when someone we have a crush on is near. In this case, Mr. Mitchell. He's Leah's idol now and the only person I've ever known Leah to openly admire. When he says things like this, she writes it down on her textbook cover with little hearts around it. She doesn't even care if Mr. Mitchell—or anyone else—sees.

"So what do you hate, Laine?" Leah asks at lunch. We're sitting at our usual table, with the regular crowd of Leah admirers.

74

"Only the things I don't understand," I say, proud of my cleverness.

"Ooh, deep," Leah says sarcastically.

"I hate snakes," Claire Watson says. Poor Claire. She isn't in Mr. Mitchell's class, so she doesn't have a clue what Leah's getting at.

"Why do you hate snakes, Claire?" Leah asks, showing mock interest.

"I don't know. They're creepy," says Claire, brushing her hair from her eyes. "They slither around and they're real quiet, so you never know when they're near you. Once I stepped on one, and I didn't even know it. I was helping my mom hang clothes on the line, and I thought I was standing on part of the rope—"

"I get it," Leah interrupts. "Never mind."

We're all quiet. Leah doesn't usually show her moody side to anyone but me. Claire looks like she's going to cry.

"So, did you guys check out Mr. Mitchell's shirt today?" Leah asks. "I think it's new." Leah always knows when to change the subject.

"It makes his eyes even greener," I say.

"He's a god," Leah breathes.

We spend the rest of lunch talking about Mr. Mitchell. We say our first names with his last, imagining what it would be like to be married to him.

The thing is we all know it's just a fantasy. He's way too old for us. All of us except Leah.

"It could happen," she says to me when we bring our trays up after lunch. "He could wait for me to get a little older. Sam says lots of older men marry younger girls. They wait for them to turn eighteen so it's legal."

"Yuck," I say.

"What?"

"Just—marrying someone so much older."

Leah shrugs. "I don't see anything wrong with it." She turns away from me like I said something to offend her.

A few days later, we find out that Mr. Mitchell got engaged. An eerie darkness comes over Leah.

It seems like weeks before she snaps out of it. We're in homeroom, and Mr. Mitchell is taking attendance, like he does every morning. He walks up and down the aisles, saying hi to everyone and making little marks in his red attendance book. As he comes up the aisle behind me, Leah lets out a gasp. I turn around.

"Leah? Something wrong?" Mr. Mitchell asks. He stops at my desk and turns his head back toward Leah.

"No," she says quietly, looking down at her desk. Her cheeks are bright red. I swear she's trying not to laugh.

Mr. Mitchell shrugs and walks past me. When he smiles, my heart flip-flops. But as he walks to the front of the room, I notice a piece of toilet paper sticking out of the waist of his jeans.

I turn back to Leah, whose whole body is convulsing in silent laughter. It's the first time I've seen her laugh since we found out about the engagement. I try to stifle my own laughter, but it's too much and I start cracking up. Luckily, we both get under control before Mr. Mitchell makes us tell him what's so funny.

That seems to be all it takes—a piece of toilet paper—to change Mr. Mitchell from God back to ordinary teacher. After that, Leah never talks about him again.

God or not, I'm still grateful to Mr. Mitchell for the friendship test. Sometimes I still look at my hand and remember the red F.F. Leah marked there all those years earlier. I think about all the things she's done to me, and I wonder why I'm still friends with her. Maybe that's what being real friends is all about—putting up with the hard lessons—both taught and learned together.

LESSON 9

It's easier to hate what we don't understand.

By the end of freshman year, Leah has definitely moved on from Mr. Mitchell. She still likes older guys, just not quite *that* old. I catch her checking out the seniors when we walk the halls. She licks her lips and looks down, trying to seem innocent and seductive at the same time. I remember similar looks she gave me in the doll closet. Her face seemed so grown-up. It's a relief to see her give those looks to boys.

The week before school gets out, Leah is in full "look at me" mode as we wait in line outside the movie theater. In a halter and short skirt, she looks about five years older than me with my usual jeans and long-sleeve shirt. She seems annoyed to have to be standing with me, like I'm cramping her style.

"If you won't hold hands with him, I will," she says to me as I bite my already chewed-to-the-skin nails. She's talking about Jeffrey Scotto, who somehow got my IM name and sent me this message two days ago:

THE ONLY GOOD THING ABOUT SCHOOL THIS YEAR WAS GETTING TO SEE YOU. WILL YOU BE AT THE MOVIES THIS FRIDAY? —JEFFREY

I love that he didn't abbreviate any words and used all capital letters, like he wanted to make sure I heard him. I printed out the message and memorized it. A *boy* likes me. A boy.

"Laine and Jeffrey sitting in a tree," Leah starts to sing as we wait in line. That stupid baby song. She sings it in an annoying little-kid voice to make sure I know how childish she thinks the whole thing is. She's way beyond "I like you" IMs.

"Are you going to let him feel you up?" she whispers in my ear.

God, I can't believe her.

"What are you talking about?" I say, stepping away from her.

"C'mon, Lainey. Are you going to let him in your shirt? Or your pants?"

"No!" My cheeks get even hotter. I feel wet under my armpits.

She makes it sound so dirty. I suddenly see us in the closet, feel her hand going—I squeeze my eyes shut and block it out.

"I doubt he'll even show up," I say, fidgeting with the hem of my shirt. I feel so self-conscious, I'm not sure I can stay standing up. Any slight breeze might make me lose my balance and I'll fall over.

Leah looks amused.

"I bet he's not coming," I say. "It was probably a joke." But I cross my fingers and hope it isn't. Jeffrey Scotto isn't even that good-looking, but the thought of a boy noticing me, liking me enough to IM me, is almost too hard to believe.

"So are you going to let him get in your shirt or not?" Leah asks, loudly enough for the people in front of us to hear.

"Would you *shut up*?" I whisper.

Just then I feel a light tap on my shoulder. I jump and turn to see Jeffrey Scotto standing in front of me.

Leah bursts out laughing. It reminds me of the laugh when we got caught with my dad's *Playboy,* only this time she doesn't sound nervous. Just spiteful.

"What's so funny?" he asks, smiling.

He seems overly pleased that I'm with Leah.

"Stand in line with us, Jeffrey, then you and Lainey can sit together." Leah's brilliant when it comes to making me feel like an absolute idiot.

"OK," Jeffrey says happily, stepping in between Leah and me.

I don't dare look at him. My tongue feels too big for my mouth.

"This movie's supposed to be intense," Jeffrey says. His voice cracks a little. When his arm brushes against mine, butterflies take off in my stomach.

Leah gives him a flirty smile. "We'll protect you, Jeff," she says.

Leah knows no one calls Jeffrey "Jeff," but of course he doesn't correct her.

When we get inside, Leah grabs Jeffrey's hand and pulls him into the back aisle. "Come on, Lainey. We'll all sit back here."

Leah walks to the end of the aisle, next to the wall. It's the darkest spot in the entire theater. Jeffrey sits down next to her, then I sit next to him.

When the movie starts, it gets even darker. I can smell Jeffrey's freshly washed T-shirt. I move a little bit closer to him, slowly, so he won't notice. Just enough so that if he moves closer, too, we might touch. But he doesn't move. In fact, I can't tell in the dark, but it seems as though, if anything, he's sitting closer to Leah.

The second preview comes on. It's for an action movie with lots of explosives that light up the theater. I try to meet Jeffrey's eyes, thinking I'll smile at him as a way to thank him for the note.

I turn, hoping my bangs look OK. That my breath doesn't smell funny. But it doesn't matter. Jeffrey's staring at Leah. She's giving him one of her looks. I only see them a second before it gets dark again, but I know I've lost him.

I sink back in my seat and sigh.

When the movie starts, there's a tap on my shoulder. My stomach flips. I don't dare to look at Jeffrey. I think his tap is a nice one. Delicate. I start to convince myself I was wrong about the look I saw pass between him and Leah.

But as I turn, I realize it was Leah tapping me. She's reached behind Jeffrey. Her arm is still over the back of his chair.

"Are you guys going to hold hands?" she asks matter-of-factly. She's chewing gum. I smell the strawberry flavor when she breathes out.

I feel myself blush again.

Jeffrey doesn't move a muscle.

"Come on, guys—what do you think movie theaters are for?"

Still nothing from Jeffrey. I'm sure he can hear my heart beating.

"Look, it's easy." Leah moves her arm from the back of Jeffrey's chair and takes his hand. "Just put your fingers through mine, like this."

Jeffrey seems as tense as I am. He stares straight ahead while she laces her fingers through his.

"Well, Laine, if you're not going to hold his hand, I guess I'll have to," she says cheerfully. She sits back in her chair, keeping hold of Jeffrey's hand.

He doesn't pull it away.

"What's your problem?" Leah says to me after the movie.

Jeffrey had muttered a "See ya" and fled as soon as we got to the lobby.

I'm not sure if he wanted to rush off to tell his friends that he'd just held hands with Leah Greene for two hours, or if he simply wanted to get away from us. One thing I'm sure of, though: I won't be getting any more messages from him. He probably thinks I'm a freak.

"*I* don't have a problem," I tell Leah. She shrugs and keeps walking.

"Why did you do that, anyway?" I ask when we get outside to the parking lot.

She turns away, like she's scoping out the scene. "Do what?"

"You know what."

"Oh, Laine, grow up." She looks around the parking lot, then at me and my pathetic outfit. She pulls at her halter to show more of her chest. "It's not like *you* were going to do anything with him."

"How do you know!"

"He's a guy."

My cheeks burn. "I *liked* him, Leah. And you ruined it!"

She laughs. "I didn't ruin anything. I saved you. If he really liked you, he would have held *your* hand. Or were you jealous?"

"*Jealous?*" I want to scream at her.

"Did you want to hold my hand, too?" She smiles at me in a sickeningly sweet way.

I'm so upset, I don't know what to say.

"Mommy's here," she says before I get the chance to think of something.

My mother is waiting for us in my dad's pickup truck. It has a big rust spot on the passenger side.

"Your dad needs a new truck," Leah complains before she opens the door.

"Maybe you should buy him one," I say.

The door creaks when she opens it.

I imagine her falling under the truck and telling my mother to step on the gas.

Leah holds open the door so I can climb in. She always does that. It makes her look like she's being polite, but really it's so she can get in last and sit by the window.

"How was the movie, girls?" my mother asks.

"I thought it was pretty good. What did you think, Lainey?" Leah pauses, but not long enough for me to answer. "Or were you too busy watching something else?"

I glare at Leah.

"What's that supposed to mean?" my mother asks.

"Nothing," I answer. "The movie was fine."

I move closer to my mom so Leah isn't touching me. I clench my teeth together and try to keep my hands from making fists.

I hate her, I think. *I hate her so much.* Screw Mr. Mitchell and his stupid tests and theories. Or don't—so what if I don't understand Leah? I don't want to! It's easier to hate. That's what Mr. Mitchell told us. That's why so many people do it, he said.

OK, Mr. Mitchell. Fine. *You* figure her out, then. Right now, I'd rather just hate her.

LESSON 10

Every joke has a little truth in it.

When school gets out, I wait to see if Leah will call me, but she doesn't. I don't call her, either. I spend most of the summer alone or hanging out with Christi when she'll lower herself to be seen with me. None of the girls from our group call me. I always knew Leah was the only one they cared about. It's OK, though. I'd rather be lonely than deal with Leah Greene or any of her followers.

When school starts again, I make a point of keeping my distance from Leah, and since I haven't run into her, I assume she's trying hard not to see me, either.

Then one Friday my mother stops Christi and me as we're heading out the door for school and tells us that Leah is coming over to spend the night.

I try to tell my mother that Leah and I aren't friends anymore, but she won't change her mind. "Mrs. Greene needs this favor, Lainey," she says. "She doesn't trust anyone else."

Christi rolls her eyes.

"Mom, *please*! Can't you call her back and make up an excuse?" I plead.

"Oh, don't be so dramatic, Lainey," my mom says. "One night won't kill you."

"But—"

"Listen," my mom says, all annoyed. "Mrs. Greene has been having a lot of trouble with Leah lately and doesn't want to leave her alone. It's just one night. If it makes you feel any better, I'm not crazy about this, either!"

"But, Mom. I haven't talked to Leah in *months*."

"Well, maybe if you two had stayed close, Leah wouldn't be so—"

My mouth drops open. I can't believe she's actually going to blame *me* for Leah's problems.

"Nice, Mom," Christi says for me. "You should be grateful Lainey doesn't hang out with Leah anymore."

"I'm just saying," my mom says, faltering. "Mrs. Greene is afraid to leave Leah alone, and I think we owe it to them after all the things they've done for Lainey over the years."

"Whatever," I say. I will never get why my mother thinks she needs to impress Mrs. Greene. Obviously, they will never be friends.

Leah finds me at my locker that afternoon. I have a flyer about soccer tryouts in my hand when she comes up behind me and peers over my shoulder. She breathes quietly in my ear.

"Hey, Lainey, haven't seen you for a while."

"Hey, Leah." I quickly crumple up the paper, but she's already seen it.

"Girls' soccer?" She smiles and narrows her eyes, then licks her lips.

I try to step away from her. "Yeah, but—I probably won't bother," I say, trying to sound casual.

"Why not? You're athletic."

"I don't know. I guess I don't want to."

She moves in closer to me so our faces are only a few inches apart. I quickly scan the hallway for who might see us.

"You know there are perks for being on a team, don't you?" she asks.

I try to move away from her again, but I'm already practically inside my locker. Her breath smells like cigarettes and mint gum. She seems different again. Meaner. I wonder when she started smoking.

"What perks?" I ask, forcing my voice to stay calm.

"The locker room, Laine? Come on—you can't fool me."

"No. Really. I don't know what you're talking about."

"Laine, you're so good at pretending you're innocent." She reaches for my hand, touching it gently before I pull it away. I drop the paper in my locker and close the door.

"I have to get to class," I say. Our eyes meet. For a second I think I see the old Leah there. The one who taught me how to ride horses and passed notes in class with me. But she quickly looks down.

"Don't give up on that tryout, Lainey. Just think of the locker room."

I start to walk away, but Leah grabs my arm.

"The locker room, Lainey. All those girls undressing in front of you? How will you control yourself?"

I feel sick to my stomach.

"Look at you," Leah says, close to my face again. "You can't hide it, Laine. I know what team you play on."

She moves even closer and whispers in my ear. "See ya tonight."

She turns and walks down the hall. As she swings her hips, her short skirt swishes back and forth, going higher up her thighs.

I lean against my locker. She's wrong. Other girls don't make me feel different. Only Leah.

But *she's* the one who did those things to *me*.

So what does that make her?

By the time Mrs. Greene drops Leah off that night, my parents have already left for a party. Christi has escaped to her room and shut the door, leaving me to welcome Leah in. Great.

She opens the door without knocking and throws her leather backpack on the floor by the door. She checks out the room. And me.

"Well, this is going to be a blast," she says sarcastically. "How the hell are you, Lainey?"

"OK," I say. "You?"

She shrugs. "I'm hungry."

"There's some leftover pizza in the fridge," I say. "Feel free to help yourself."

She wrinkles her nose as if I offered her leftover

meat loaf, but she goes into the kitchen anyway. I don't follow her.

I watch TV in the living room, waiting for her to come back out. But she doesn't. After a while, I hear her voice through the kitchen door. I turn down the volume on the TV.

"Come on," she says. "Why don't you come over and party? Her parents aren't even here."

I walk to the kitchen and poke my head through the doorway. Leah's sitting at the kitchen table with her feet propped up on it, one of my father's antique bar glasses in her hand.

"Just a minute," she says when she sees me. She lets the mouthpiece slide down below her chin. "May I help you?" She takes a sip of her drink.

"What are you drinking?"

"Gin and tonic. Want one?"

Who is this person? To a stranger, Leah probably looks about eighteen or nineteen, not sixteen.

When I don't answer, she takes a long drink and turns her back to me.

"So will you *please* come?" she asks the person on the phone. She laces the cord of the old phone my dad restored through her fingers as she talks in a fake whine.

"I bet I could cheer you up." She pauses as the other person says something, then giggles.

I leave her there and find Christi in her room, studying French.

"*Oui?*" she says, looking up.

"Leah's drinking Dad's gin."

Christi stops smiling. "Perfect. When will Mom and Dad be home?"

"I don't know."

"Lainey?" It's Leah calling from the kitchen. "I'm still hungry!"

Christi looks worried.

"She was asking some guy to come over and party," I tell her.

"Crap." Christi gets up, annoyed. "Can we just lock ourselves in here?" She's kidding, but I would have been up for it.

"Lai-ney! Where are you?" We hear Leah climb the stairs and make her way to my room. "Lainey?"

"I'm in Christi's room!" I call back reluctantly.

"Hey, guys," she says from the hallway. "I didn't even know you were here, Christi. What were you doing? Hiding?" She has one hand behind her back. In the other is a full glass of gin and tonic. She's even cut a lime for it, like my parents do at their parties.

"I'm trying to study," Christi says. "What are *you* doing?" I can tell she's trying to sound authoritative, but she isn't really pulling it off.

"If you're the babysitter, maybe you could make me something to eat?" Leah takes a long drink from the glass.

"There's leftover pizza in the fridge," Christi says. "Didn't Laine tell you?"

"Why don't you like me, Christi? You've never liked me, have you?"

"What are you talking about?"

"I make you nervous, don't I? Just like I make Lainey nervous. Why do I make everyone so fucking nervous?" Leah walks closer to us as she speaks, keeping her hand behind her back. Her lips are wet and shiny. Her cheeks are pink. She smiles as she walks toward us, swaying a little, then takes another drink.

"How much have you had, Leah?" I ask.

"Get over it, Laine. God, you're such a prude." She smiles, though. "Or at least you'd like to be, wouldn't you?" She looks at Christi, then winks at me.

I move closer to Christi.

Leah stops in front of us.

"What do you want?" Christi asks.

"I want you to make me something to eat." Slowly,

94

Leah starts to bring her hand from around her back, still hiding whatever she's holding. She smiles mischievously. The ice cubes in her glass clink.

"Fine." Christi moves past us and starts down the hall. Leah follows her. That's when I see what she's holding behind her back. It's a tiny paring knife that she must have used to cut the lime for her drink.

"Leah!" I yell before I can even think what she's doing.

Christi stops at the top of the stairs and turns around. "What is it?" she asks.

Leah stands between us, still facing Christi. "Oh, this?" she asks, showing Christi the knife.

"What the hell is that for?" Christi asks.

"What do you think it's for?" Leah says. She touches the tip of the knife to the inside of her arm, slowly running it down to her wrist. The now half-empty glass spills a bit as she does it.

"Jesus!" Christi yells.

"Relax," Leah says, taking the blade away so we can see a speck of blood form a tiny bubble at her wrist. She smiles at us.

"God, Leah. Put it down or give it to me," Christi says. "It's not funny."

"You want it, Christi? Or do you want some of this?"

Leah holds out her glass to Christi. Christi reaches for the glass, but Leah quickly pulls it away and chugs the rest of it. "Sorry, you'll have to make your own. I'm sure you wouldn't want something I put my mouth on, anyway."

"Give me the knife, Leah," Christi says. "You're drunk. You're going to hurt yourself."

"C'mon, Leah," I try, finally finding my voice again. "This is dumb."

"Like you care," she says. She touches the blade to her wrist again, spilling a remaining ice cube on the floor.

"I—I do care, Leah. What the hell?"

"Put the knife down. Now," Christi says, stepping toward her.

Leah keeps the knife pressed to her wrist.

"Why are you doing this?" I ask.

"Would you really care, Laine? Would you care if I did it? Or would you be relieved?" She runs the knife across her wrist again, leaving a tiny red line.

Without thinking, I step forward and snatch it out of her hand.

"I'm calling Mom and Dad," Christi says.

"Oh, please." Leah rolls her eyes. "It was only a joke.

You don't think I'd really do it, do you?" She starts to head down the stairs as if nothing has happened.

"You passed the test, Laine!" she calls back over her shoulder. "I guess you still fucking care after all."

"What a psycho," Christi says. She walks back to her room and slams the door, leaving me standing in the hallway alone. I look down at the small knife in my hand. It has blood on it. Mine.

I don't know why, but I don't want Christi to see, so I go to the downstairs bathroom. Leah is there, fixing her hair. I ignore her and open the cabinet to find a bandage.

"Oh, fuck!" she says when she sees my hand. "Are you OK?"

"Do *you* care?" I ask.

A car horn in the driveway interrupts my cold stare.

"Oh, shit," Leah says. "I've gotta go. I'm really sorry, all right? It was only a joke. Seriously, are you OK?"

Behind the makeup she actually looks concerned. Even scared. Maybe.

The car horn blows again.

"I've gotta go," she says.

She runs through the dining room, grabs her bag, and shuts the door hard behind her.

I creep to the open window and listen through the screen.

"When I honk, you get your ass out here!" a guy's voice yells. It sounds way older than someone in high school.

I listen for Leah's response, but I don't hear anything. The sting in my palm starts to throb as I try to peek out at them.

"Just get in!" the voice shouts. A door shuts. Tires squeal as the car tears out of our driveway.

I go back to the bathroom and finish fixing my hand. Back in my room, I try to stay awake until she gets home, but the next thing I know it's morning and Leah isn't here.

When my parents ask where she is, I tell them she left with someone last night, but I don't know who. I keep my hand in a fist and don't say anything about the knife. Christi shakes her head at me when my parents aren't watching, but she doesn't tell, either.

Mrs. Greene pretends not to be mad at all of us when she shows up at the house a few minutes later and finds out that Leah's gone. My parents keep apologizing, saying they were out late and didn't know Leah was missing until just now.

I don't know why Christi and I don't tell them about the knife. I don't think it occurs to either of us that Leah would really hurt herself. Not seriously, anyway.

We were so stupid. Of course it wasn't a joke. It was a warning.

LESSON 11

Sometimes the good-byes you
want the most are the hardest.

Leah and I spend the next few weeks avoiding each other. The long Columbus Day weekend can't come soon enough. I spend the whole time in my room reading with Jack curled safely at my feet. Christi feels sorry enough for me to actually invite me to go shopping with her and her friends, but I pass.

I dread going back to school the following Tuesday, but it's a waste of time because Leah isn't there. She's gone.

As the weeks go by and she doesn't return, more and more rumors spread about where she went. The ones I've heard so far are: she dropped out to go to modeling school; she transferred to a fancy all-girls' finishing school; her parents sent her to a girls' military school to straighten her out; she transferred schools because she's already slept with all the guys in this school; and she got pregnant.

I haven't spoken to Leah since the knife incident, so I have no idea what's true. And even though I'm selfishly relieved that she's gone, I worry. To feel better, I try to convince myself that if anything really bad happened, Mrs. Greene would tell my mom.

Some days, I still feel her watching me. Taunting me. Sometimes when a pretty girl walks by me, I can almost hear Leah's wet whisper in my ear, "Checking her out, Lainey? She's cute, isn't she?"

But Leah's not here anymore. It's just me, beating myself up.

After Leah's comments about soccer, I decided to prove her wrong by joining the team after all. I'm not afraid of the locker room. I'm not checking anyone out. Actually, I like getting ready in the locker room, listening to the gossip as we dress for practice, like I'm part of a group again, even if I'm outside the circle. It's not all that different from the group of fake friends I had with Leah.

"I heard our new uniforms will be in Friday," Jen

Thomas says as she laces up her cleats before practice. She's talking to Carrie Winters. They're both juniors.

"I hope mine's the right size," Carrie says. "Remember how tight my top was last year? God, I didn't even need a sports bra. I swear Ms. Sawyer does it on purpose so she can check us out."

Ms. Sawyer is our coach. She's openly gay and has a partner, so I doubt she's interested in them.

Jen pushes out her flattish chest. "She's not checking *me* out, that's for sure. Unless she likes little boys."

"Maybe little girls," Carrie jokes.

I wish they'd shut up.

"This school is so whacked," says Jen. "I can't wait to get out of here."

"No shit. Speaking of getting out, have you heard about Leah Greene?"

My ears get hot.

"She moved, right? That's old news. And good news, if you ask me."

I try to pay attention to my cleats, but I'm sure my head is leaning way too close to them as I hang on every word.

"No, she didn't move. She's just not coming back *here*," Carrie says.

"Why not? Is she too good for us? God, she and her sister are so stuck-up."

I act busy stuffing things in my backpack so they don't think I'm listening.

"Actually, I heard that Leah tried to kill herself," Carrie says.

I drop my bag and look up. Jen stops brushing her hair. "Seriously?"

"Yeah." Carrie almost smiles, like she's proud to know this top-secret news.

I pick up my backpack again and put it on the bench. My hands are shaking.

"Maybe sleeping with every guy in the senior class last year got to her conscience," Jen says, brushing her hair again.

"Who knows. Why is it all the rich, beautiful girls who do crap like that? I mean, she has everything going for her, so what does she do? She sleeps with every guy on the planet and then tries to off herself. She probably just did it for attention." Carrie stands up and looks at herself in the mirror. She tucks a few loose strands of hair back into her ponytail.

Jen rolls her eyes.

"I heard Leah transferred to private school over at

Sheldon," says Carrie. "All the rich fuck-ups end up there."

"She's just like her slutty sister, Brooke," Jen says. "They think they're so much better than everyone else."

I see Leah pressing the knife against her wrist and look down at the scar on my palm. I squeeze my hand shut again. I feel dizzy. I pull off my cleats and put my school clothes back on. No one seems to notice or care. I shove my practice clothes in my backpack and stand up. The cement floor feels like it's swaying underneath me. I wobble as I step forward. Carrie gives me a funny look.

I walk out of the locker room, out of the school parking lot, and away. Nobody tries to stop me.

It's cold and windy outside. The sidewalks seem empty, even though they aren't. I walk looking down at the pavement in front of me.

The cold stings inside my ears and makes my head pound. I walk faster, finally ending up downtown, in front of the glass door of my parents' antique store.

I stand outside looking in. My father is talking to a customer. They can't see me out here in the dark.

I hold my hands in fists inside my jacket pockets. The air is cold and damp-feeling. But I can't go inside. I'm supposed to be at practice. I'm supposed to be happy Leah is gone and out of my life. But I can't stop thinking about the last time I saw her, pressing that knife to her wrist. Asking me if I would care. Telling me I passed a test I didn't even know I was taking.

The woman shopper inside the store turns toward the door. I step aside quickly. The tiny customer-warning bell jingles as the door closes behind her. Her heels click steadily down the sidewalk as she walks away.

The store is quiet. I watch my father smooth his hand over a polished table. Then he walks to the back of the store, and I can't see him anymore. When he turns out the store light, I see my reflection in the glass. It startles and sickens me at the same time.

I turn around and lean against the cold store window.

Leah tried to kill herself.

Leah tried to die.

I try to remind myself of all the mean things she's done to me, but in the end it doesn't matter. With Leah, it never did. Even from the very beginning. No matter how much she hurt me, I always came back. All she had to do was reach for my hand and pull.

I feel what I think is an emptiness in my stomach. I turn back toward the store window again, but as I see my pale reflection and the darkness behind me, I realize that what I've really been feeling is loneliness.

I'm crying when my father puts his hand on my shoulder.

"Laine, honey. What are you doing here?"

It's the first time since I was really little that I've cried out loud. He puts his arms around me and squeezes me into his down parka. It smells like wood polish, and I cry on it. My hands are still shoved in my pockets, and with his arms around me, they're stuck there. So I just stand and let him hug me. I'm glad he doesn't ask what's wrong. He seems to understand somehow that I don't want him to. And, anyway, where on earth would I begin?

When I can't cry any more, we drive home. I can't eat, even though my mother tries to make me. My father gives her a look that tells her to leave me alone.

I go to bed and put the covers over my head. I think back to that night when Leah came over for the last time. How she looked at me and Christi as she held the knife to her wrist, like we were pathetic losers. How she laughed at us. For a second, I had wished she would just do it—plunge the knife in and get out of my life. But the feeling vanished when I heard the sound of the car horn and the stranger's angry voice and I watched Leah disappear into the night.

Before I know it, it's morning, and I have to go back to school and face all those girls who think they know Leah. Who hate her because they don't understand.

I spend the following day at school walking from class to class feeling numb and alone. I rub the scar on the inside of my palm, trying to remember the details of that night. Was Leah really warning us? Was that supposed to be her cry for help?

When I get home from school, I decide to call her.

Mrs. Greene answers the phone.

"What a surprise, Lainey!" she says in her high-pitched voice. "So good to hear your voice. We've missed you!"

While I wait for her to get Leah, panic slowly creeps into my chest. What do I say? I heard you tried to kill yourself, and I'm calling to find out if it's true?

"Hey, Laine," Leah says.

I'm surprised to feel glad to hear her voice.

"Hi," I say.

There's a long pause. Maybe this wasn't such a good idea.

"What's up?" she finally asks. "Decide to miss me?"

"Um. Well. Of course I miss you," I lie.

"Of course?"

I should hang up.

"I was just calling to see—to see if you're OK."

"Why wouldn't I be?"

I should've known she wouldn't make this easy.

"Um. Well. I heard this rumor."

"A *rumor*?" she says in mock surprise. "About *me*? That's shocking."

"Yeah. Well. I guess it was only a rumor."

Because you sound like your usual old self.

"What was it?"

"Oh. Nothing. It was dumb."

"What was it?" she says, more demandingly. "Let me guess. I got pregnant?"

"No."

"I got kicked out of school?"

"No."

"I had an affair with one of the teachers? I got caught using drugs?"

"No. It wasn't any of those things."

Please stop.

"Then what? I've heard them all, Lainey. You can't surprise me."

Fine.

"They said you tried to kill yourself."

I listen to her breathe. I wait. I count her breaths. Six, seven, eight—I can't take it anymore.

"Leah? It's not true, right?"

"Of course not," she says. But her voice sounds different. "God, Lainey. You're so gullible. I'm glad you give a shit, though—I really am. I could use a friend like you at my new school. But, Laine, we've both moved on, you know?"

This time, I'm the one who doesn't say anything. Is this really it? Is Leah letting me go for good?

"Yeah. Um, OK," I finally say. "Sorry to bother you. I'm glad it was only a rumor."

"Thanks, Lainey. Hey, have a good life."

She hangs up before I can say good-bye for real.

I don't know how many times I've wished I'd never met Leah Greene. I don't know how many times I was sure I hated her.

I should be thrilled to be set free at last.

So why do I feel so empty?

LESSON 12

Some lies are for your
own good.

For months after I talk to Leah, I have the same dream about her. She's in a black sports car with a faceless man. She lifts her arm to wave good-bye. As she does, blood starts to gush out of a slit in her wrist. She's crying. I try to open the door to let her out, but the car is moving, pulling away from me, down a black dirt road. Leah keeps waving at me. And now I can't tell if she's waving good-bye or gesturing for me to come after her. The blood starts to cover the window until I can't see her face. I run after them, but the car disappears. Then I wake up, sweating. Feeling sure the rumors were true.

*   *   *

One day I'm home sick from school with a bad cold. I'm lying curled up in a ball on the couch with my favorite old quilt wrapped around me, watching old *Real World* episodes, when the doorbell rings. I waddle to the door, still wrapped in my quilt. I assume it's my mother coming home from work to check on me. She's always coming to the door with her hands full, pressing on the doorbell with her elbow so someone can come help her. I swing open the door without looking to see who it is first.

Standing there in a shiny sweat suit that looks brand-new, and certainly hasn't been sweated in, is Mrs. Greene.

"Oh, Laine!" she exclaims when she sees me. "This is grand!"

"Hi, Mrs. Greene," I manage to say to her heavily made-up face.

"Are you under the weather or something, Laine? I didn't expect to see you."

I nod.

"Oh, I'm sorry. But I'm glad, too. Not that you're sick, I mean. But that you're here. I've been meaning to bring this to you for weeks. But, you know, things get busy. I've been carrying it around in my purse for days, and today I *finally* remembered to do something about it." She's made her way inside, closing the door behind her.

It occurs to me that we've probably never been alone together before, and it feels a little odd.

Mrs. Greene rummages through her large black patent-leather purse.

"Ah," she says. "Here it is."

Before I have time to guess what it could be, out comes the nesting doll that Sam gave me all those years ago. As soon as I see it, I can almost smell that night: the candles, the food, the wood polish on the floor.

"It's your nesting doll, Laine! Remember?"

"Yes." But I don't hold my hand out. I just look at the doll sitting quietly among Mrs. Greene's perfectly manicured fingers.

We're still standing in the hallway. My head feels like it has doubled in size, and I can't close my mouth because I have to breathe through it.

"You must have left her at the house, Laine. And then forgotten about her? Anyway, when I was reorganizing some of Leah's and Brooke's things, there she was. And I thought, well, that was Laine's doll! Leah tried to tell me that you gave it to her, but I know Leah. Sam meant for you to have it."

She presses the doll into my hand.

"Thanks," I say. I try to imagine Leah being caught in a lie, but I just can't do it. Leah is the best liar ever. She told me once it was OK to lie as long as you asked God to forgive you right away afterward. Sometimes I thought I knew when she was lying because she'd pause for a minute and I thought maybe she was saying a quick, silent prayer.

"It's a shame you two aren't friends anymore. But I guess you grew apart. That always happens in high school, when you take different classes and things."

I nod, feeling the line across the doll's middle with my finger.

"My goodness were you two inseparable! Remember, Lainey?"

"How does Leah like her new school?" I ask. I look up at Mrs. Greene to show her I really do want to know.

Her face is grayish, her makeup cakey. She seems older than I remember.

"Oh, well, Leah's a little too big for her britches these days. Says she wants to quit school because she isn't learning anything. Ah, Laine, I never should have started her in kindergarten a year late. But I wasn't ready to let go of her! I think she hated being almost a year older than all her classmates, though. I think it was hard on her, even though she was always such a good student. But she developed so early, anyway, and then—well, you know. Leah has always looked a lot older than she is. When we took her out for her thirteenth birthday, the waiter thought she was eighteen! He couldn't take his eyes off her."

She says the last bit proudly. I see Sam dancing with Leah and Brooke in the living room, watching their bodies, while Mr. and Mrs. Greene smile proudly. I feel ill. I want to hurl the doll across the room.

"You should see her now, honey," Mrs. Greene goes on. "She thinks she's going to be a *model*. I wish I had the pictures from her portfolio to show you. We had them done at a studio in Boston. The photographer told us she was a natural. So of course now she thinks she can just quit school and become the next supermodel."

Just like Sam said, I think.

"Well," she says with a sigh, as if it's all too much to think about. "And what about you, sweetie? What have you been up to? Thinking about college yet?"

But she doesn't wait for me to answer. "Oh, I had such high hopes for Leah. For Brooke, too. You know about Brooke, don't you, Laine?"

I shake my head.

"She's going to go to school to become a court stenographer."

"A what?" The doll feels heavier and heavier in my hand as I try not to remember that night.

Please, Mrs. Greene. Just go away.

"A court *stenographer*. It's the person who types out what people are saying in a court case. You know. Like a trial. She's really excited. Thinks she's going to be able to witness all the interesting cases. *I* think it would be boring. At least she might meet some lawyers, though. You know, she really is pretty."

I manage to smile, even though I desperately need to blow my nose.

"So, a touch of the flu? I hear something's going around."

I sniff.

"And here we are still standing!"

"Oh, I'm sorry." I feel like a child standing in my pajamas with my blanket. When I move aside, she heads straight for the kitchen. I didn't even know she knew where it was. I follow, my blanket trailing behind me, wondering what I'm supposed to do next. I've never spoken to Mrs. Greene for this long in my life.

"Can I make you some tea, Laine?"

In my own house? "Um . . . OK," I say quietly. I place the doll on the kitchen table and sit down.

Mrs. Greene turns the doll so she's facing me before

she walks to the stove to start the kettle. She hums while she searches for and finds two teacups and the tea bags. She seems peculiarly happy. Like she's trying too hard. Mrs. Greene was always so proud of how beautiful her girls were. Still are. Maybe too proud. *If you've got it, flaunt it,* she'd told them. But at what price?

We drink our tea while the doll watches us.

"Do you know why it's called a nesting doll, Laine?"

I shake my head.

Mrs. Greene reaches for the doll and separates her. She pulls out each doll, lining them up in a row as she goes until she gets to the last doll. Then she puts them all back inside each other again. "Each doll nests inside the next biggest one. And the largest one of all keeps the others safe, like a mother hen."

"That makes sense," I say, taking a sip of the tea. It tastes better than the way my mother makes it—it has lots of milk and sugar. I wonder if she makes tea like this for Leah.

As soon as I finish, Mrs. Greene gets up to leave. When I thank her for bringing the nesting doll, she gives me a close hug. Her breasts smoosh up against me, but it doesn't make me feel bad, like I'd imagined when I saw her do it to other people, though never Leah or Brooke. I don't think I've ever seen her hug them.

From the window next to the door, I watch her hurry across the driveway to her new white Cadillac. She waves as she pulls away. I wonder if I'll ever see her again.

I go back to the kitchen and find the nesting doll still sitting happily on the table.

I hate that Mrs. Greene took her from Leah. I hate that Mrs. Greene must have found the doll and confronted Leah about it. It would have reminded Leah about that night and my broken promise. I can still see the strange glance between Sam and Leah when she took the doll from me the next morning. How he almost seemed to know she'd do it, and so it had really been a gift for her all along. But mostly I can still hear the sound of her quiet cries in the dark the night before.

I take the doll up to the doll closet and throw it inside. The doll breaks apart when it hits the floor. I shut the door before the pieces rattle to a stop.

LESSON 13

*New friends don't always
help you forget old ones.*

By the end of my sophomore year, I pretty much give up
on ever having any real friends. I'll get through this tor-
ture they call school, and then I can go live as a hermit
someplace.

Only just as I make up my mind to live my life in
exile, Jessica Lambert comes up behind me and tells me
I have a pen mark on my shirt. I try to cover the spot by
holding my books in front of it.

"It's not a big deal," she says. "That happens to me
all the time." She smiles at me.

"Thanks," I say, looking at my shoes.

I've known Jess, which is what everyone calls her, since grade school. But we've never been friends. Leah never liked her for some reason. Leah made all the decisions about who would be in our "group." None of those girls ever felt like real friends to me. I knew they only talked to me because of Leah. And Leah knew it, too. Sometimes I think Leah liked it that way.

Jess and I both play the clarinet in band. For Christmas, my father gave me an old clarinet he found at a flea market. He fixed it up and insisted that I try to learn how to play. I wasn't crazy about the idea of being a band geek, but once I tried playing, I liked it. I liked making noise without using my voice. Besides, if I'm going to be alone the rest of my life, who cares?

A few days after the shirt incident, I sit next to Jess at practice. She smiles at me and says, "Hi."

"Hi," I say back, a little too friendly.

This is the extent of conversation number two. But at the next practice, we sit beside each other again. This time she nudges me when Mrs. Hathaway, the band director, claps her hands and tells us we're all brilliant.

"Must be deaf," Jess whispers.

I snicker.

Two practices later, Jess asks if I want to share stands with her.

"Sure," I say nervously. But when I put my music away to share hers, we realize she plays second clarinet and I only play third, and both sets of music won't fit on the stand.

"Oh, well," Jess says. "We can still push them together. That way Hathaway can't see us write notes."

Hathaway? Notes? Apparently, Jess has decided we're friends.

I slide my stand next to hers so our music folders touch and Hathaway can't see us. Jess gives me a satisfied smile.

After practice a few days later, Web Foster is waiting in the hall for Jess. I didn't know they were friends, but it's obvious they're close by the way Web grins at her when he sees us. He doesn't seem surprised to see me with Jess. He even knows my name and says hi.

The next day we're sitting in chemistry, and Web sends Jess and me the same note.

I dare you to scream as loud as you can at 10:05.

We both look over at him like he's crazy, but he winks and points to the clock.

I don't think any of us will really do it, but as I

watch the minute hand slowly making its way to the five, I decide I'm going to go for it. It's the end of the school year. What's the worst thing that could happen? What do I have to lose?

As the second hand nears the twelve, we exchange looks and nods. Then, just as the hand clicks onto the twelve, I take a deep breath and let out a "Wooh!"

Jess and Web echo my own pathetic, but victorious, howl.

When we stop, the room is deadly quiet. We look at one another, our faces bright red. I feel like I've just lifted a huge weight off my chest, and I'm smiling like a nut. I've never done something like this before. Leah would never do it. She'd say it was totally lame. She'd probably roll her eyes and say how juvenile we are, which is basically what the rest of the class does. No one looks at us. Mrs. Fiske, our teacher, just says, "Enough!" But no one in the class even acts like it was an odd thing to do.

After class, the three of us meet in the hall and burst out laughing.

"That was the weirdest experience I've ever had," Jess says.

"Jess, you live a boring life." Web sighs.

"But nothing happened," I say. "No one did anything! We didn't even get in trouble!"

"We freaked them out, that's all," Web says. "It was beautiful, wasn't it?"

"Yeah," Jess and I say at the same time. Then we all crack up again.

I have passed their initiation test. I have friends. I wonder what Leah would say to that.

LESSON 14

Forever is the rest of your life.

Just when I finally make friends, they desert me. Two weeks after the scream, school vacation starts and Jess and Web go away. Jess goes to Maine with her parents, who run a dive shop there all summer. Web's parents are making him go to private school in the fall, so he has to go to their summer-school program before he can enroll.

I'm alone again.

I decide to work in my parents' antique store. Mostly I dust and polish things. My dad plays fifties music off the restored jukebox because he thinks it makes customers feel nostalgic. Within two weeks, I'm walking around with Buddy Holly and Fats Domino songs in my head. It is so pathetic. I'm convinced that I'm a complete failure and will be a hermit the rest of my life after all, humming to the tune of "Ain't That a Shame."

But then Jess IMs me and asks if I want to come spend a weekend with her.

I write back in all capital letters: YES!

She sends back a smiley face.

When I step off the bus, she hugs me close. I hug back and glance over her shoulder at the small wharf and quaint little shops by the water. As we embrace, I feel odd, like people are looking at us. I pull back quickly, but Jess doesn't seem to notice.

"I can't believe you're here," she says. She has a dark tan. Something about her is different. She looks great. Maybe it's because she seems so much more relaxed than at school. Maybe it's just the tan.

"We're gonna have a blast!" She grabs my backpack off my shoulder and drags me up a narrow street. Her parents' summer place is right in town, a little apartment over the dive shop. Jess's room is a tiny, renovated attic painted white with a round window with a view of the ocean. There's a single bed under the eaves with milk crates stacked on top of each other for a side table.

"It's not much, but we won't spend time in here

anyway," Jess tells me. "C'mon. Get your suit on and we'll hit the beach."

She pulls her tank top up over her head and begins to unfasten her bra. I quickly turn away. My cheeks are hot.

"What's with you, Laine? We're both girls," she says matter-of-factly.

I try to laugh and fumble through my backpack for my bathing suit.

I turn my back to Jess while we both get dressed. I'm sweating.

Please don't let me have any weird feelings.

Please don't let her look at me.

Please don't let her be like Leah.

I dress as fast as I can, trying to hide myself as I do.

But when I turn around, suit on, Jess is already in her bikini, not even paying attention to me. I tell myself to get a grip. I put my T-shirt and shorts back on over my one-piece and we head out.

We spend the day on our towels, pushing our toes into the hot sand as we watch the waves. Jess rates the guys that walk by us and I say higher or lower. Usually I say higher. Jess tells me I should be more picky. But I doubt *any* of the guys we see would be interested in me. A few of them check out Jess, but their eyes pass right over me.

The first night, we walk down the pier and buy cheap jewelry. Jess wants to get a tattoo, but you have to be eighteen. The whole time we're walking she keeps brushing up against me. The first few times, it surprises me and I flinch.

Jess isn't Leah, I tell myself. *She isn't.* Is it too much to ask to have a normal friend?

I'm starting to think there is no normal. Not for me.

That night in Jess's room I spread my sleeping bag out on the floor.

"There's room for you in here," she says, patting the bed.

My body tenses.

No. Not another Leah.

I shake my head. Too confused to speak.

"Oh, phew. I was hoping you'd say no." She laughs. "This bed is *way* too small." She takes a folded quilt from the foot of her bed and arranges it under my sleeping bag. "At least let me give you some cushion. I'll trade if you want."

"No, that's OK," I say, giddy with relief. "I'm fine."

The next night we walk out on the beach. We lie down next to each other on a blanket Jess brought and look up at the stars. A group of people have a bonfire party going down a ways, but we don't join them. I watch the half-moon above us and listen to their music. Every few minutes there's a collective laugh.

"School's gonna suck with Web gone next fall," Jess says.

"Yeah," I agree.

"It sucked enough with him there last year. You two are, like, my only friends."

I don't answer at first. The two of them are plenty for me. So I say "Yeah" again.

She rolls over on her side to face me. "You used to have lots of friends in elementary school and stuff, though. Weren't you and Leah Greene best friends or something? What ever happened to her, anyway?"

One of the bonfire people squeals and I hear splashing. I close my eyes and see myself with Leah and the other girls, thinking we're so special. We were awful.

"She went to private school," I say. I sit up and move to the edge of the blanket so I can push my feet into the sand. "After she left, the girls we hung out with kind of drifted apart."

I don't admit to her that they were never really my friends. It sounds so pathetic.

"Oh, yeah. Right," Jess says. "Now I remember. She

was really screwed up, wasn't she? Didn't she try to kill herself or something? I always wondered if that rumor was true. Was it?"

"I don't know," I say quietly.

She sits up and joins me at the edge of the blanket. She nudges me with her shoulder.

"I'm glad I got to know you, Laine. I always thought you were such a snob." The side of her thigh touches the side of mine. "Now I know you were just weird."

She elbows me.

I move away a little so our legs don't touch.

"I was only kidding," she says, moving closer again.

"I know," I tell her. But I still don't want her touching me. All this talk about Leah. If she could see me now, she'd probably think I was a total loser, hanging out with Jess. Or she'd tell me I was attracted to her. But I'm not. I don't feel anything. Only scared.

I stand up and walk toward the water. I stop where the sand gets hard and let the ice-cold waves reach my toes. With each wave, my feet sink deeper into the sand. It reminds me of when Christi and I were younger and we pretended we were sinking into quicksand.

"You better pick up your legs, Laine!" Jess calls to me. "I'm not getting my feet wet to save you!"

But just then some guy runs by us and starts puking

into the water. I turn and run back to our blanket. Jess and I pack our stuff and take off, giggling.

Jess walks me to the bus stop the next day. Before I get on the bus, she wraps her arms around me and squeezes me tightly. "I'll miss you, Lainey," she says in my ear. Her breath is warm and wet and familiar.

I jump back.

She looks confused. "Have a safe trip."

What just happened?

"Thanks," I say, trying to sound normal. "For everything. I had a great time."

I heave my backpack up over my shoulder and climb onto the bus. From my window, I watch her standing on the curb. She waves and holds her hands up, pretending she's typing. "Send me a message," she mouths.

All the way home, I feel her breath in my ear.

When we first met, Leah asked me if I knew what forever really meant.

"Of course," I told her. But I didn't.

"It's your whole life," she said. "Friends forever is friends always. No matter what."

I didn't know what she really meant. Maybe she didn't, either. Maybe she meant that some friends stay with you even after they're gone, haunting you forever.

LESSON 15

If he really likes you, he'll hold your hand.

Two weeks before school starts, Jess IMs to say she's back and asks me to go with her to Web's for a reunion.

Web's house is gigantic, like the Greenes'. He rushes out the front door and wraps his arms around me and kisses me on the cheek. "Hey, girlfriend," he says.

His arms feel good, holding me tight. He looks surprisingly pale, compared to Malibu-tan Jess.

"Me, too," Jess says, joining our hug.

Their arms pull me against them, and I don't know where to put my face. It ends up smooshed against Web's neck. He smells like expensive soap.

"I have a present for you guys," he says, breaking away.

We follow him inside. He gets his backpack from a large hall closet and puts it on the floor, then pulls a bottle of Kahlúa out of it. He smiles, flashing us his freshly white-stripped teeth. "Got milk?" he asks, grinning.

"It's your house," Jess says. "Do you?"

He rolls his eyes at her and carries the bottle and his backpack down a long hallway. Jess follows, skipping behind him like a little kid.

"Where are your parents?" she asks as she follows.

"Away," he says over his shoulder.

I walk behind them, loving how normal it seems to them that I'm here, too.

We take a gallon of milk and three plastic cocktail glasses filled with ice into Web's bedroom and shut the door. We sit cross-legged on Web's bed in a sort of circle.

Web makes the drinks. We forgot a spoon, so he cups his hand over the top of his glass after he's poured the ingredients in and shakes. He licks his palm when he's done and smiles at us. "Who's first?" he asks.

Jess trades her empty cup for the full one. Then Web makes two more.

"Cheers!" Jess says.

131

We click cups and drink. It's cold and thick and sweet. The liquid gently burns in my chest.

Web and Jess pretend to be at a cocktail party, sticking out their pinkies as they drink, so I do it, too.

As I sit on the bed with them, I feel like I'm inside myself. Like I'm this miniature me standing inside my head, looking out through my eyes as if they're windows. I want to tap on the glass. To shout. But I'm trapped inside. It feels like something else is controlling me, making my arms move, my mouth swallow.

Don't screw this up, I tell the outside me.

I take another long drink.

Web turns on his stereo. We sit and drink and smile and drink.

"It's so good to be back together," Web says.

"Did you miss me?" Jess asks.

"Of course," Web says. "I missed both of you. Did you miss me?"

"Of course!" Jess says, leaning up against him.

"Of course," I say, mimicking Jess.

I tip my glass back and finish it off. I feel dizzy and deliciously happy. I lick the sweet off my lips.

Web and Jess lean back against the headboard. I slide over next to Web so I can lean against it, too. We stretch our legs out in front of us. Web starts to make his feet move to the music. Jess and I copy him. Our feet look like six little dancers moving in sync. We don't say much. I vaguely remember Web getting us more drinks and the room feeling hazy.

The next thing I know, I'm waking up in a bed with a wastebasket next to my head and the taste of throw-up in my mouth. Something warm leans against my back. It's dark in the room. I don't know where I am at first, but I recognize Web's bedspread. The warm thing against me moves and makes a grumbling noise.

"Oh, God." I sit up. My heart and head throb in unison. I've never felt this ill in my life. I try to check my watch, but it's too dark to see. I scan the room for Web's digital clock. The orange numbers read 9:15.

Web's hand touches my shoulder and gently pulls me back down beside him.

He rubs my back softly in tiny little circles, sending shivers down my belly and between my legs. I know the feeling, but it is so much better this time, without the fear. Or shame. I will him to roll me over and kiss me, even if my head is splitting.

Look at me now, Leah, I think automatically, happily.

"Are you OK?" Web asks softly.

I nod, trying to replay the night and figure out how we ended up in this bed together. I still have all my clothes on, but I hope something happened. Anything. I love the way Web smiles. The way he looks at me. The way he pays attention to me. Being next to him now seems almost too good to be true.

Web's fingers travel up and down my back.

Don't let him be another Jeffrey Scotto, I tell myself. I hear Leah's voice, *If he really liked you, he would have held your hand.*

"That feels so good," I say, breaking the silence. *Keep doing it.*

The fingers move in circles.

"You feeling OK?" Web asks softly.

"Mmm-hmm," I say, ignoring my pounding head. I want so badly to roll over and kiss him, but I can only imagine what my breath must smell like if I was sick.

His hand moves to my head, and he gently brushes my hair away from the side of my face. I will him to put his hand on my shoulder and roll me over to face him.

But then there's a moan from the floor.

"Ick!" It's Jess. "The fairies have been making sweaters on my teeth."

My heart sinks.

"How'd you get down there?" he asks.

He moves closer to me and kisses the back of my head before pulling his hand away.

Quick! Roll over and kiss him back! I scream at myself. But I can't. Not with Jess here.

When she moves in next to us, I realize Web was just making room for her when he got closer to me. He rolls over and I hear him kiss her, too.

These were "just friends" kisses. "Just friends" back rubs. Just friends. Just nothing.

Thank God I didn't try to kiss him and make a total fool out of myself.

If he really liked you . . .

Web stands up and stretches. "Breakfast or dinner?" he asks.

Jess and I get up slowly, groaning and pretending our heads hurt even more than they do. In the kitchen, the three of us sit at the table, drinking coffee and eating Pop-Tarts. Jess gives me a long list of excuses I can tell my parents for not calling and telling them I would be late. Web chooses which ones he thinks have the best chance of working. We talk as if we've always been friends. At first I hope Web will give me a special look that says maybe we could be more than friends, but I don't get one. After a while, I forget to watch for it. I just feel happy that somehow I made it to this place, this table, with these people.

As they talk and laugh with me, I watch them as if they are strangers and my only friends in the world all at the same time.

LESSON 16

You can't escape your past.

The Saturday before school starts, Web calls me.

"We have a date tonight," he says.

My heart flutters. All week I've been reliving that moment on his bed, his body spooning mine, even if it was a "just friends" spoon.

"What about Jess?" I ask.

"She's at her grandparents', remember? We don't have to do *everything* together, do we?"

"Well, no, but I thought—"

"I'll pick you up at around eight, and we'll have some fun before we go in."

"Where are we going?" I ask.

"It's a surprise. But bring your dancing shoes."

"But—I don't do the dance thing."

"You do now."

My stomach is a mess the whole day. Fun before we go in. Dancing. Oh, God. I play a few CDs and practice in front of the mirror, but I look like a total dork. It's hopeless. Maybe I can pretend I don't feel well when we get there so I can just sit and watch him.

Web picks me up in the Mini his parents gave him for his sixteenth birthday. It smells like him. We drive forty-five minutes to a club near Web's new school.

We park in a dark corner of the parking lot. Web cuts the motor, then reaches for a paper bag in the backseat.

"Every time a car pulls in, we have to drink," he says, slipping a new bottle of Kahlúa out of the bag. "SUVs are two drinks."

Each time we pass the bottle, our fingers touch and a spark shivers through me. I hope he feels the same thing. But if he does, he doesn't show it.

We keep drinking. It gets harder and harder to force it down. Finally, Web hands me a piece of spearmint gum.

"Begin now," he says. He watches the clock on his cell phone and makes us chew for exactly seven minutes.

"OK, we're good to go," he says when our time is up.

"Why seven minutes?"

"Lucky number. That's how long it takes to get rid of alcohol breath."

"Really?"

"Trust me."

He winks and I melt.

Despite Web's theory, I try not to breathe when we sway/walk to the door. It's a good thing it's dark.

Web pays the bouncer for both of us as if this is a real date.

Inside, the place is packed. It smells like Gap cologne, sweat, and hair spray. I recognize a few people from school, but most of them I don't know. Web nods to a group of guys I've never seen. They're probably from his new school.

The music is blasting. I'm so buzzed, I barely feel my feet touch the floor as we make our way to the bar. There's a huge line for drinks, which is dumb since all they serve is Coke and fake mixed drinks. As we stand there, it seems like the wall behind the bartender is moving.

Web says he's going to run to the bathroom. He hands me a ten and says to stay in line. I wait for a few minutes before I realize I have to go, too. Like, right now.

When I step out of the stall, I find a free sink and splash my face with cold water. Please don't let me get sick. Not here.

When I check myself in the mirror, I cringe. I look like hell. My cheeks are blotchy, and there's a brown Kahlúa stain on the front of my shirt. Very attractive. I'm surprised the bouncer even let us in, it's so obvious I'm drunk.

I splash more cold water on my face, then look up in the mirror again.

"Hi, Lainey."

My heart drops to my stomach.

She's standing right behind me.

"Leah. Hi!" I try to sound friendly, but I think I sound more terrified. I don't know if I'm supposed to turn around and hug her, like normal long-lost friends would. But even if I wanted to, she's up so close behind me I can't really move. My hands are trembling.

She smiles from behind me at our reflection in the mirror, and I try to smile back.

She's taller and seems much older than me. Her hair is longer, too, and her face is more defined. She's even more beautiful. She really could be a model.

I put my hands on the counter to steady myself,

feeling even uglier than before. The way I've always felt when I'm with Leah.

"It's nice to see you, Lainey," she says. "What's it been, like, a year?"

She moves to the sink next to me and washes her hands. Her deep-red fingernails match her lips. I try to get a look at her wrists, to see if the rumors were true, but she keeps her hands palm-down somehow, and I can't get a good look.

When she straightens, she checks me out.

"You're a little pale, Lainey," she says in a suspicious way. "What have you been up to?"

I roll my eyes and try to look cool. She knows the answer.

"Excuse us," some girls say, annoyed that we're hogging the mirror. Leah steps behind me again and frees up a sink. My heart beats hard against my chest. My head is throbbing.

"You look good, Laine," she lies.

Our eyes meet in the mirror. She has dark eyeliner on with glitter eye shadow. Her red lips are covered with a shiny gloss. She looks way too old and sophisticated to be at a bar on teen night.

"Uh, thanks," I say. "You look good, too."

We both know *good* isn't the right word to describe either one of us. She is beautiful. And I am not.

She's standing so close, I feel her breath on the back of my neck. I wore my hair up in an attempt to look more feminine, but with Leah behind me with her perfect curvy body, I feel anything but. Just like old times.

The other girls leave, rolling their eyes at us. Some new ones squish in. I just want to get out of here, but Leah's blocking my way. I pretend to tuck a wisp of hair back into place as if there is really anything to do in front of the mirror besides loathe my appearance.

"It's nice to see you out, Laine," Leah says. She flicks her hair back over her shoulders. "Are you here with friends?"

"Just one. My friend Web."

She raises her eyebrows, but before she can make a comment, I ask her who she's with.

"My boyfriend," she says. She rolls her eyes when she says it. "Speaking of which, I better get going. He freaks out when I'm gone too long."

I think of my dream and the faceless man driving her away. Her blood on the window. I don't let myself look at her wrists again.

The sink next to us opens, and she steps in, leaning

142

close to the mirror to put on another layer of shiny red lip gloss.

"OK, well, it was great to see you again," I lie, stepping away from the sink while I have a chance.

"Hang on," she says. "I'm coming, too."

Before we get to the door, she takes my arm to stop me. I try to shrink away from her, to swivel around her, but she leans in close and squeezes my arm harder. I smell her cherry lip gloss mixed with some kind of alcohol.

I turn my head away. Our faces are so close, I swear she could kiss me. As I turn, her wet lips brush against my ear and she whispers into it.

"Remember when we used to mess around, Lainey?"

I push away from her, afraid someone has heard.

"What are you talking about?" I glare at her and rub the gloss off my ear, regretting all the months I've felt sorry for her, worried about her. God, she hasn't changed at all.

"You remember," she whispers.

"I have to go," I say.

She follows me out to the dark hallway.

I turn and face her. My head is pounding, and I feel like I'm going to be sick. "What do you want?" I almost hiss.

"I know it bothers you, Lainey, but there's nothing wrong with it."

I glance toward the men's room. "I need to find Web," I say.

"Just wait, Laine, OK?" She reaches for my shoulder, but I shrug her hand away.

"I'm sorry, Lainey. I was just messing with you."

Just messing with me. Just messing around. Just messing up my entire life.

She sighs dramatically as she steps closer to me. "God, Laine, you're so uptight. You have to get over it. We were just kids. We were just experimenting. Every-one does it."

Then why do you torment me about it?

I wish I dared to say the words out loud.

Her face softens. "Hey, truce, OK?" She reaches for my shoulder again, but I step back.

"Come on, Lainey. It's just a joke. Look. I'm glad I ran into you. My mom told me she brought back that stupid doll a while ago. I tried to tell her you wouldn't want it, but she kept insisting Sam had given it to you, not me. I was going to call you after, but I forgot."

She fidgets with the strap of her top. "You remember that doll, right?"

"Yeah," I say, remembering how I threw it into the

closet. "I was surprised when your mom showed up with it."

I don't know how we're suddenly having this casual conversation after what just happened. All I want to do is get away from her. But I stay.

Leah rubs her wrists and looks down the hall toward the dance floor, like she's looking for someone. "Fucking Sam, that prick," she says.

I peer down the hall, too, wondering who she's watching out for.

"What do you mean?" I ask. "He let you take the doll that day. If you want it back, you can have it."

She presses her temples with her fingers and leans against the brick wall next to us. "I didn't want the fucking doll," she says. "I didn't want—"

She stops.

"Fuck it. Never mind."

"Didn't want what?" I ask. "What happened with him, anyway?"

She looks away from me and out toward the dance floor again. "Forget it. It's over now."

Her eyes look glassy, like she's trying not to cry.

"God, Leah. What did he do to you?"

Her bottom lip drops. Our eyes meet.

Just tell me, I think.

"Hey! I thought you were gonna wait in line!" Web comes bouncing over to us.

Leah fake-smiles at him.

"Hey, Leah," he says, like they're acquaintances but not friends.

Then I remember. They'll be at the same school this year.

"I'll see ya later, Lainey," she says, quickly grasping my wrists and squeezing. But when I give her a concerned look, she kisses the air at me and transforms from the girl about to cry to the girl about to pounce.

"Have *fun*," she says sarcastically, nudging her head at Web. Then she saunters off confidently, as if nothing happened.

"What's her problem?" Web asks as she struts away.

I shrug. I can still feel her hands on my wrists.

"She was in one of my summer classes. I think she was doing our English instructor. He was always checking out her ass."

"Leah was in summer school?" I can't believe straight-A student Leah would ever need to take special classes.

"Yeah, but she hardly ever came. I think she and the instructor had their own *private* lessons." He smirks,

146

and it annoys me. It annoys me that he did it, and it annoys me that I even care. I don't know exactly what Sam did to Leah. But it doesn't give her the right to treat me this way. Screw that.

"C'mon. Let's go dance," I say. Clearly, I must still be drunk, since I would not in a million years suggest this at any other time. But now I just want to show her. I want to show her I'm with Web now. I have a friend. Maybe a boyfriend.

Web takes my hand, and we shove our way onto the crowded dance floor. It doesn't really matter that I don't know what I'm doing. It's so packed with people, we're all like one massive body waving back and forth. Web and I put our hands in the air and sway, our stomachs pressed up against each other. I look around for Leah, but I don't see her.

But just because I can't see her doesn't mean she can't see me. *Look at me,* I think. *Look at me with a boy. I'm over you. I'm not what you think.*

I press closer to Web, our pelvises touching. He smiles at me and rocks into my body. I want to kiss him, but I don't dare. Could we be an *us*? I'm so light-headed, I can barely feel my feet or hear the music or feel the sweat I know is beading on my forehead.

I will him to kiss me, but instead he looks down at me and smiles, as if this is the best fun he's ever had. As if I am his best friend.

Later, when we're leaving, Web holds my hand so we don't get separated in the sweaty crowd. We slowly inch toward the exit sign while people push and bump against us. Then someone grabs my other wrist. I panic, thinking I'll get separated from Web. I try to pull away, but the person holds tight. I don't need to look down at my wrist and see the long, graceful fingers, the deep-red nail polish, to know who it is. She manages to squish between two people, pulling my arm as if it's a tow rope. She motions to Web and smiles.

"Nice try," she mouths at me. Then she lets go and disappears back into the crowd.

I squeeze Web's hand harder and let him pull me out of there. But Leah's *nice try* lingers in my ear, and I can't stop wondering what she meant. Did she know I was trying too hard to make him like me? Did she know I was trying to show her I was into guys? Or, worse, did she know Web would never be attracted to someone like me?

LESSON 17

If you look close enough,
you'll see the truth.

The first week back at school, Jess tells me that one of
Web's friends is having a huge party Saturday night.

Before the party, I go to Jess's to get ready. She makes
me change my shirt and wear a tank top. She tightens
her lips and looks at my chest like she's disappointed.
She sticks out her own and admires it in the mirror.

"Maybe if you stood up straighter," she says, jutting
her chest out ever farther so her boobs almost touch
the mirror.

I let my shoulders slump forward again. Whatever.
Like I want anyone looking at my chest. Like I would
know what to do if they did.

We sneak a few drinks from her parents before we leave, just to loosen up. Jess's parents are always having big parties, so there's plenty of alcohol in the house, and her parents never notice when some goes missing.

When we get to the party, I already feel buzzed. There are about six or seven cars in the driveway. We see Web through the huge kitchen window that overlooks the front walk. We have no idea who lives here, but it's like a mansion compared to our own houses—even Web's. We pause outside to check out the kitchen scene. Web is doing shots with some guys we don't recognize.

As soon as we step inside, Jess grabs Web's shot glass and downs one, then refills the glass and gives it to me. I sniff it.

"It's raspberry Chambord," he says. "You'll love it, Lainey."

I smile at him, hoping to see something in his eyes that says he likes me back. Nothing.

He pours the shot glass three-quarters full, then tops it off with some cream from a purple carton. I tilt my head back and fill my mouth with the sweet stuff. I swish it around before I swallow. It's delicious.

"*Mmm*," I say.

"Told ya." He winks at me, and I actually blush.

We finish the bottle and then switch to vodka and Sunny Delight. It doesn't compare, but by then I am willing to drink anything.

Most of the night is a blur. I spend it standing against a wall in the living room, watching people dance and feel each other up at the same time. I don't know how many people are here. Lots. I don't know any of them.

Jess disappeared with a guy about twenty minutes ago, confirming that our time in Maine was just my freakish paranoia. Leah always told me I was a bad judge of character. She was so convinced everyone had a story. Sometimes when we were at a public place like the beach, she'd whisper each person's secret life as they walked by. Whenever I made something up, she'd shake her head and tell me I was a bad people reader.

"You're just afraid to look closely," she'd tell me. "You don't want to know the truth about people."

I'd look again at all the people walking by, but she was right. I was afraid to look too closely.

I take one last look around for Jess before I go to the kitchen for some more juice. Straight juice this time.

The light is off when I get there, but when I flick it on, someone yells, "Cut the shit!" I shut it off again and walk quietly to where I think the fridge is. When I open the door, the light clicks on and I see two bodies pressed together, leaning up against the marble-top counter.

"Fuck sake!" a familiar voice says. I quickly grab the juice and swing the door shut. It's Web.

I turn to leave, but I can't help looking to see who he's with. Web looks away, burying his face into the person's neck. It's the guy who gave us the raspberry stuff.

"Sorry," I manage to mutter. I stumble through the room, leaving Web and the stranger in the dark.

I don't know why I'm shaking. Like I'm the one who was caught, not him. But *caught*? It's not like he was cheating on me. It's not like . . . It's not like he was ever going to like me more than as a friend.

I should have known. I should have looked closer.

I replay the night at the bar in my head, with me trying to get Web to kiss me. And Leah, right before we left, smirking and saying, "Nice try." I thought she was talking about my pathetic attempt to look like I was with a guy, which now seems infinitely more pathetic.

She knew the whole time. Of course she knew. They were in summer school together. Web said something about being able to be himself there, but I was too clueless to know what that meant.

I manage to push my way through the living room

of dancing bodies, down the hall, and out a sliding-glass door to a huge stone patio. I sit down on the ledge overlooking a pool made to look like a pond.

How could I be so stupid? How could I not have known? Everything makes sense now. Maybe I should be glad. He wasn't attracted to me because he's gay, not because there's something wrong with me. So why am I not relieved?

"Hey," a whispery voice says behind me.

I turn and see a guy I don't know but recognize from inside. I think I saw him dancing.

"I'm Lucas."

"Hi," I say. "Laine."

"Strange name."

"Yeah."

He sits down next to me.

"You have amazing eyes," he says.

Really?

No. I know it's a lie.

The jug of juice sits next to me on the bench. I wish I had more to drink.

He takes a long swig from his own red plastic cup and smiles at me.

"Can I kiss you?"

Before I answer, he leans forward and presses his

lips against mine, forcing them open with his tongue, which is cold from whatever he's been drinking. Coke and something stronger.

This is not the first kiss I imagined.

I see Web in the kitchen again, being held.

I squeeze my eyes shut tighter and concentrate on kissing the stranger back.

He puts his arms around me and slides me closer so our chests touch. He moves his hand from my back toward my front at my waist. I'm still trying to figure out the kissing thing, thinking, *Oh my God oh my God oh my God, I'm Frenching a total stranger,* when his fingers find their way under my tank top.

I feel like one of those cartoon characters when they hit their head and little birds spin around like a halo. I am so wasted. And yet every sensation in my body feels very, very, very alive. His thumb presses under my bra and finds my nipple. *Oh my God oh my God oh my God.* It feels good. Scary, but good. Very good.

The sliding door wooshes behind us.

"Lainey? You out here?" It's Jess. She calls out innocently, even though I know she sees me.

The hand slips out of my shirt at the same time the tongue leaves my mouth. Lucas—that was his name, right?—pushes away.

154

"Uh, later," he says. He doesn't even bother to smile.

I wipe my mouth with the back of my hand as he dashes off, leaving me to wonder how the hell that just happened.

"Nice," Jess says, nudging her head in the direction he fled. "Sorry to interrupt, but you looked like maybe you needed to be saved."

"I guess," I say. The excited feeling oozes out of me and off into the shadows. Why do I feel like I've been caught doing something bad?

"You seem"—she inspects my face—"sad." She sits down next to me.

I shrug. "I'm stupid—that's all," I tell her.

"Stupid how?"

I shrug again. And then, I don't mean to, but I start to cry. Only a little, but enough for her to notice.

"Hey," she says. She moves closer to me and puts her arm around me. "Was that guy bothering you?"

"No." I wipe my eyes with my wrist. I'm an idiot. First for being so amazingly clueless about Web, then for letting a complete stranger feel me up.

"I didn't—I didn't know about Web."

"Know about him how?"

"I didn't know."

"Know what?"

155

"I walked in on him and another guy."

"You mean you didn't know he was *gay*?" She looks shocked.

"Yeah."

At first I think she's going to laugh, but as she sits and thinks, I see her put it all together, and instead of gloating, she squeezes me to her. "Oh, Lainey. That sucks," she says.

I rest my head on her shoulder and cry quietly. Not because I'm sad that Web and I really don't stand a chance, but because Jess is here, being a friend the way I always imagined a friend should be.

For the first time, I don't feel uncomfortable when she touches me. I just feel comforted.

When I recover, we open the orange juice and pass it back and forth. Jess tells me about the guy she hooked up with in some bathroom, and I tell her about my five minutes with Lucas.

The sliding door opens again, and Web steps out, all disheveled. We crack up.

"What?" he says, but we just get hysterical.

"Move over." He squeezes between us and takes a long swig from the juice. "Great party," he says. "Next weekend, it's at my house."

LESSON 18

There is more than one type of friendship test.

Web's first party is a blast.

It's easy to make up an excuse for staying out all night. All I have to do is tell my mom I'm staying at Jess's. Sometimes there are benefits to having your mom think you're a loner freak.

There's this picture of me, Web, and Jess on my screen saver. We're wasted, but to the average clueless mother, we simply look really, really happy. I'm sure it makes my mom ecstatic to see me in a photo with *friends*—and I'm even *smiling*.

At the party, someone from Web's school has managed to score a small arsenal of serious stuff from their parents. It's nasty-smelling, but Jess is good at finding ways to hide the smell—even the flavor—when necessary. We play drinking games to force down the first few chugs. After that, the taste gets better.

By the end of the party, people are totally out of control, getting sick in the bathroom, hooking up in any open space available. I keep an eye out for Lucas, but I don't see him. Not that I want to be with him, but . . . well, maybe I do.

I keep replaying that time on the patio with him and wish it had been Leah who walked out to see us instead of Jess. I can almost remember his hand on my breast, and Leah's words from way back, when she first told me about getting felt up and I didn't know what it meant. It felt about as romantic as she described—someone rubbing my tit. But it also felt pretty good.

I look around for something more to drink, even though I don't really need it. Jess and Web find me in the kitchen.

"Come on," Jess says. "Escape walk."

"What about all these people?" I ask. Web shrugs, like he doesn't understand what the big deal is, leaving a bunch of drunken strangers in his house.

It's dark and cold when we step outside. Fall is coming fast this year. Web brought a travel mug with orange juice and vodka with him. The three of us pass it back and forth as we walk to the gazebo behind his house.

We sit on the floor so we can't see the house, only the silhouettes of the trees around us. The music from inside feels far away.

After a while, we hear cars starting as people begin to leave. I swear Web's keeping track of how many, wait ing until he thinks everyone has left.

When we finally go back inside, everyone's gone except for a few people passed out on the floor and on the two couches in the living room.

Jess and I follow Web up to his room. He pulls off his sweatshirt and pants and then draws back his blankets.

"Looks like none of us are getting lucky tonight, girls. Care to join me?"

Jess strips to her tank top and panties and crawls in. I hesitate, standing at the edge of the bed.

Web pats the empty space next to him. "It's OK, Laine. You know you're not my type." He smiles the way I love, even though it still hurts. I take off my pants but keep my long-sleeve shirt on. Then I crawl in. Web spoons me from behind, his warm arm draped over me. He breathes steadily in my ear. It feels good, and horri- bly hopeless.

"'Night, guys," Jess says from the other side of the bed.

Web is already snoring softly.

"Good night," I whisper. I close my eyes, letting my hot tears slip down my jaw.

A few weeks later, Web has another, even bigger party. Web's house is the perfect place to have parties because his parents are never home. Most weekends they go to their place on the Vineyard. And in November they'll go to Florida and only come back north for Thanksgiving and Christmas reunions with Web. Other than that, they think the house is unoccupied, with their perfect son at boarding school making them proud. Ha.

I've been drinking steadily for about an hour before I find my way to the bathroom in the master bedroom. Jess and I have put an "out of order" sign on the door so people will think it's broken and we'll never have to wait in line.

When I'm done, I open the door and step into Web's parents' bedroom. Someone has turned off the lights. I don't think anything of it, but as I step into the dark, I feel a hand grab my wrist. At the same time someone whispers *"Shhh"* in my ear.

My heart races.

"Nice party, Lainey," she says.

"Shit! God, Leah. You scared me."

She sucks in her breath. "Nice to see you, too."

"What are you doing here?" I ask. My heart pounds in my chest the way it does whenever I'm scared. The way it does when I'm with Leah.

"I followed you."

I don't tell her that's not what I meant. I would have thought she'd consider herself too cool for partying with people her own age.

"Sorry I scared you," she says. She walks over to a side table and clicks on a reading lamp, then sits on the bed. The low light casts a dark glow over her skin. She has on a silk tank top and definitely no bra. She pats the space next to her for me to sit down.

I stay standing, still recovering from the shock of seeing her again.

"I won't bite," she says. She shifts on the bed. She's wearing a sheer skirt that shows the shape of her perfect thighs through it. I look down at my loose jeans.

I try to act casual when I walk over to her and sit down.

"So, how've you been, Lainey?"

"I've been fine," I say, matching her fake cheerfulness. "How about you?"

She smiles and pushes her blond hair away from her face with the back of her hand. I catch a quick glimpse of her wrist but don't see a scar. Maybe she only tried to slit one wrist. Maybe it's the other one.

"I'm fine, too," she says.

"How's Brooke?"

"Great. Never been better. She's fulfilling her dream of becoming a court stenographer."

"Yeah, your mom told me about that. That's cool." I relax a little, relieved the conversation isn't about me. Or us.

"Whatever." She starts to play with her silver thumb ring.

I wait for her to ask me how Christi is, but she doesn't.

"So, is this your thing now, Lainey? These parties every weekend?"

"Yeah, pretty much," I say.

"*Hmm.* Well, I'm glad you have friends," she says. I can't tell if she's being sarcastic or sincere. Her voice sounds quiet now. Sad.

I try to read her feelings, but her face seems vacant. She's wearing glittery blue-tint eye shadow with liner that makes her eyes look happy, even though it's obvious she isn't. She still looks beautiful underneath it all, but it's not the beauty she used to have. She seems empty.

When our eyes meet, she half smiles at me.

"Did you come here with friends?" I ask.

She looks away from me and pushes her hair behind her ears again. "Nah," she says quietly. "My boyfriend."

She pulls her skirt down tight against her thighs. If I didn't know better, I would think she was nervous. But Leah doesn't get nervous. Not around me.

"Where is he?" I ask.

She shrugs. "Trying to score something, most likely. What about you, Lainey? You have a boyfriend yet?" She slides closer to me. "Or do you still prefer girls?"

I'm not going to let her do this again.

I stand up and get ready to walk away, but then I turn around. "Not that it's any of your business, but I prefer guys, Leah. Guys. Sorry to disappoint you."

"Why would that disappoint me?"

"You know why."

"I have an idea," she says. She stands and walks over to me, blocking the space between me and the door. "Why don't you prove it to me?" She takes my hand. "Kiss me right now and see if you feel anything. Prove to me that you only like guys."

I pull my hand away. "I don't have to prove anything. I already know."

"No, you don't," she whispers.

"Yes, I do," I say back.

I walk around her to the door and flick on the overhead light in the room. Leah squints at me in the bright light.

"Why do you always do this?" I ask.

"Do what?"

"You know what. You act all nice, and then you get weird and nasty."

"Nasty? Oh, come on. I'm only goofing on you, Laine. God, you're so sensitive." She flicks her hair over her shoulder. "Why is it so important to you to like guys, anyway? Guys are losers. There's nothing wrong with liking girls, ya know."

"I never said there was anything wrong with it. I just don't."

"Then why are you so upset?"

I want to hit her. "Because you won't drop it! After all these years, you keep hanging it over my head. You're so convinced you know me. You don't know anything."

"I know it still bothers you."

"Maybe you're the one it bothers!" I say back. "If what we did means I like girls, then what about you? Why do you have a boyfriend?"

She shrugs. "It was different for you than it was for me."

"What? How? How would you know?"

"It just was. Trust me."

I shake my head.

"Aw, Laine. You need to get it through your head that no one cares what you are. Just be happy for once in your life and stop worrying about it. I'm only trying to help you."

"How is this helping? You're the one who said we should move on, Leah. So why do you show up to torment me? I'm trying to be happy, but you keep wrecking any chance I have!"

She honestly looks hurt at that.

"You call this happy, Lainey? You look pretty lonely to me."

"I have friends now, Leah. Friends that I made on my own."

"Really? Where are they?"

I feel myself deflating. Jess and Web *are* my friends. I know they are.

"Where are *your* friends, Leah?" I shoot back. "You're so worried about my being happy. What about you?"

She smiles at me, but it looks like it hurts. I don't know why, but I feel like I'm going to cry.

"Just leave me alone from now on, OK?" I say quietly. "Just stay away from me." My voice cracks a little.

"Lainey, wait. I'm sorry, OK? I really am trying to help you."

"If you really want to help me, stay away from me."

"Lainey, just—just wait." She comes toward me slowly and reaches for my shoulders with both hands. "There's something I have to tell you," she says quietly. The points of her fingertips press into my shoulders.

"Don't touch me," I say.

She lets go, then frowns, as if now *she's* the one who's going to start crying.

"OK, OK," I say, hating myself for giving in so fast. "What is it?"

She moves closer to me.

"I want you." She laughs and steps back.

"Fuck you." My cheeks burn. I hate her so much. I've hated her before, but nothing like this.

"Lainey, wait. I'm sorry. I couldn't resist."

I keep walking.

"Please wait? I really do want to tell you something."

166

But I don't wait. I don't even look back. When I step into the hallway, I almost bump into Jess.

"Hey," she says. "Everything OK?"

"Yeah," I say, looking back to see Leah standing in the middle of the room, smiling at us. "Fine."

Jess makes a concerned face and puts her hand on my shoulder. "You sure?"

I nod, wondering how much Jess saw and heard. I know Leah can see Jess touching me. I can almost feel her smirk. *Go ahead,* I think. *This is what* real *friends do.*

"Come on," I say. I don't look back again. We find Web in the kitchen, drinking with some guys from his school.

Jess grabs his hand and tells him we all need to take a walk.

Outside, the air is still pretty cold, but we make our way to our gazebo and huddle together.

"What's up?" Web asks.

Jess looks at me.

I don't say anything.

"Leah Greene was giving Lainey shit in your parents' bedroom," Jess says.

"That psycho? What's she doing here, anyway?"

I squeeze my arms around myself.

"Lainey, what was it about?" Jess asks.

I shake my head. "Nothing," I say.

"It didn't seem like nothing."

"Why, what happened?" Web asks.

I feel myself slipping away from them.

"Lainey?" Jess asks.

What did she hear? What did she see?

Tell them, I think. *Just tell them.*

I open my mouth.

Tell them.

"Ancient history," I say. "I'm fine. Really."

I know they don't believe me, but they each put an arm around me and hug me from either side.

"We'll protect you from her," Web says.

Jess gives me another squeeze. "Definitely."

I close my eyes and force myself not to cry.

What would Mr. Mitchell say?

Did I just fail the friendship test?

Or did Jess and Web just pass it?

LESSON 19

Some markers really are
permanent.

During Thanksgiving break Web's parents are home, so he doesn't have any parties. He tells Jess and me he's taking us on a mystery date. He says to dress warmly and picks us up at my house. The only other hint of where he's taking us is the big wool blanket folded up on the backseat of his car. Jess raises her eyebrows and yells, "Shotgun!" before jumping into the front passenger seat.

Web hands her a thermos as he pulls out of my driveway. "Careful, it's hot."

"*Mmmmm*, you'll like this," Jess says to me, handing the thermos back between the front seats.

I'm sure it's some concoction with more alcohol than anything else, but when I take a sip, it's just hot chocolate. Rich, perfect hot chocolate. When I swallow, the warmth travels down to my chest and stays there.

Twenty minutes later, we're at a state park we used to go to on field trips in elementary school.

Jess and I follow Web along a well-worn path to a large pond surrounded by trees and picnic tables and a few grassy spots, though the grass now is brown and the ground is frozen. Web spreads out the blanket on the hard ground. We watch some joggers and dog walkers make their way around the pond. The wind is cold on our faces, but it feels good. After a while we lie back and try to soak up the warmth of the sun.

"I see a turtle," Web says, squinting behind his dark sunglasses.

"That's not a turtle; it's a whale," says Jess.

The sun warms my face. The clouds are like paintings slowly sweeping across the blue sky. I don't see a turtle or a whale.

"I see a small horse chasing a bigger one," I say.

"Where? I can't see that!" Jess shades her eyes with her hand.

The horse clouds glide in front of the sun and cast a shadow over us and the blanket.

"Your horses just turned gray," Web says. He stretches his arms out and pulls us closer to him. His down parka smells like outside and feels soft against my cheek.

In the distance a child screams excitedly. I sit up just as a little girl runs past our feet, followed by another girl who looks about the same age. The first one has two long braids that stick out from under a bright red hat. She reaches a tree and yells, "Safety!"

But the other one ignores her and grabs her arm. "Got you," she says.

"No fair!" the long-haired one whines.

"Baby," the other one says. She has short hair that's almost bleached white. Instead of a hat, she has a fuzzy pink scarf wrapped around her neck. The ends trail behind her regally. She turns to walk away, but the long-haired one shouts, "Wait!" and runs to her. She slips her mittened hand into the other girl's, and they walk away, swinging their joined hands up and down.

"They're cute," Jess says. She's propped on her elbows, watching the girls skip away.

From behind, they look familiar. I can almost feel Leah's hand in mine. I look down at the scar on my palm and imagine the shadow of the letters she wrote all those years ago in permanent marker. When I glance up again, the girls dash behind another set of trees.

"You two are way cuter," Web says.

Jess nestles her head back onto his chest.

"Lie down with us, Lainey," Web says.

They smile at me, and Web holds out his free arm. Somehow when I lean back down, my head winds up resting in his armpit. His black coat is warm from the sun and cozy against my face. But instead of feeling comforting, it's smothering. I roll away from him and watch the trees where the girls disappeared.

"What's wrong?" Web asks.

What's wrong? What's wrong? I wish I knew. Leah's voice burns in my ears. *You call this happy, Lainey? You look pretty lonely to me.*

I shake my head. "Nothing," I say. I know it's not true. But it should be. I picture the three of us—me, Web, and Jess—going to all those parties, IMing one another, passing out together in Web's bed, and getting up early to have breakfast and coffee and gossip about the night before. It all feels like a movie I watch but I'm not really a part of.

If Web and Jess are such good friends, why do I feel so lonely? If Web and Jess are such good friends, why can't I tell them the truth? The questions pool in the back of my throat. I know the answers all come down to Leah. And me. And what we did. And that I just can't bear the thought of Web and Jess knowing.

A flow of hair swings out from behind a tree and disappears. A girl giggles in the distance.

I sit up again and pull my knees to my chest. I wrap my arms around my legs.

"You sure you're OK?" Jess asks, sitting up, too.

Web joins her, so we're all sitting on the edge of the blanket, watching the woods beyond the pond.

Web's shoulder touches mine.

"It's just that . . ." I try. "Those girls . . . they remind me . . ." The words choke me. I swallow them and let them slide down into my chest. "Never mind. It's nothing."

Web reaches for my hand and makes me let go of myself. His hand is warm and firm in mine. I will him not to let go. Ever.

The long-haired girl comes tearing out from behind the trees with a huge grin on her face. Her braids bounce against her puffy red coat.

The short-haired girl isn't anywhere to be seen.

I know the trick. If the long-haired girl is winning, the other one will simply say she isn't playing anymore. I want to tell her. I want to tell her to go find a real friend.

But who am I to give advice on friendship? If I was a real friend, I would tell the truth. I would give Web and Jess the ultimate friendship test.

I study my hand in Web's, how his fingers curl around mine like a promise.

I open my mouth to try again, but I still can't figure out how to start.

Web eases his hand out of my grasp as he lifts it to shade his face from the sun. His eyes meet mine. They tell me he knows I'm hiding something.

"Well, we're here for you, Lainey. Right, Jess?"

"Definitely."

The three of us all lie back down again. I close my eyes and tilt my head to the sun.

The little girls scream and giggle and sound happy as they run off again.

"This is heaven," Web says softly.

"You're a sap," Jess tells him.

"Thank you," I say to the sky. Because I believe them. I believe they are here for me. Even if I can't tell them the secret.

We're quiet, listening to the happy noises around us. I concentrate on all the good things surrounding me at this moment. But Leah is in the shadows. She always will be. Our secret keeps her there. Friends forever.

LESSON 20

All secrets come out eventually.

By spring break Web's parties are legendary. When I show up for his "Big Break" party, there's already a line of cars parked down the street. People are spilling out of the house and into the driveway. Web's parents will be coming back from their winter place in a few weeks, so Web says he has to make the most of these final days of freedom.

Web and Jess are already drinking when I get there.

"Lainey!" they yell as soon as they see me. They both seem totally buzzed already. Jess introduces me to a bunch of her friends from Maine who drove all the way here for the big event. I feel their eyes on me as they check me out. I wonder what Jess told them about me. She puts her arm around my waist and squeezes.

"Ready for some fun?" she asks.

Before I can answer, Web kisses me on the cheek, then pushes a beer in my hand.

As he does, one of Jess's friends starts chanting, "Chug! Chug! Chug!" Pretty soon everyone in the room joins in.

Web rolls his eyes but smiles, too. He nods, urging me to do it.

I put the cup to my mouth and try not to breathe in and smell the bitter beer. The first drink is always the hardest. I force myself to swallow a mouthful, but the chants get louder. I swallow again. And again. Some of the beer drips over the side of the cup and slides down both sides of my chin. When I put the cup down, it's empty. Web wipes my chin with the back of his hand as people give a halfhearted cheer, then go back to what they were doing. Web fills my cup again and winks at me.

"Great party, huh?"

I make myself nod.

A guy from Web's school comes over and kisses Web on the back of the neck. Web gives him a hug but doesn't introduce me. I force myself to smile at them before I step back, out of the way.

I take a sip of beer and turn to where Jess was standing, but she's gone. The room's already crowded, with a steady stream of people shoving their way in. I move to a corner where I can be invisible. I recognize a few people from some other parties, but a lot of them I've never seen before. After a while Jess appears again with her friends from Maine. I lift my hand and start to wave her over, but she turns before she sees me and gets swallowed up by the crowd. I don't go after her. I take another long drink instead. I haven't felt this lonely in a long time.

After a while, my invisible corner starts to cave in on me. Someone steps on my foot and doesn't bother to say sorry. I try to move aside, but my shoe is stuck to the floor and almost comes off before I can unstick it. I make my way through the kitchen and out to the living room. It's even more crowded.

When I get to Web's parents' room, there's a group of guys sitting on the king-size bed passing a joint around. It's hard to breathe, and I have to go to the bathroom. People figured out the "out of order" trick, so I have to wait in line. I try not to smell the sweaty kid in front of me who is hitting on the girl in front of him. Everyone seems to be swaying. It takes forever for people to go to the bathroom, and I'm sure I'm not going to make it.

When it's finally my turn, I step inside, close the door, and lean against it. I look around the once-immaculate bathroom. The toilet is clogged. Someone has thrown up in the bathtub. The floor is wet with either beer or pee or both, and I have to put my hand over my mouth to keep from throwing up. The scene is so depressing, so pointless, I start to cry.

Someone knocks on the door. My head spins as I straddle the toilet, afraid to touch the seat. Even though my bladder feels like it's going to burst, nothing happens. Someone pounds on the door. "Hurry the fuck up in there!"

I pull my pants up and avoid looking in the mirror as I splash cold water on my face to wash away my tears.

I open the door and shove my way through the people I don't know and escape outside to the gazebo. By then I can't hold it any longer, so I squat behind a bush.

Instead of going back inside, I sit alone in the gazebo. It's cold, but I can't bring myself to go back to the party.

"It's not safe to be out here all alone, you know."

I jump at the sound of her voice coming from the darkness. My heart races as she steps into view. I try to see her face, but the shadows hide her eyes, even when she steps up onto the gazebo and sits across from me. I can't tell in the dim light, but her hair seems blonder than before. She's wearing a low-cut, sparkly pink halter with a tight and very short black skirt.

I hug my arms around myself and try to breathe.

"Hi to you, too," she says.

"Hi," I say quietly.

She shifts on the bench so she's sitting sideways to face me. The light from the house shines across her face as she turns. I look away from her dark eyes.

"So, does your friend know you pee in his yard?" she asks.

Was she *spying* on me? I hug myself tighter. "What are you doing here?" I start to stand up to leave.

"Relax, Lainey. I only came out to say hi."

Yeah. Right.

"How long have you been here?" I ask, feeling my stomach tighten. "I didn't see you inside."

"My boyfriend's been doing some business in the driveway. It was boring, so I thought I'd take a walk.

That's when I saw you come out the back door and water the rosebush. You didn't get stabbed by any thorns, did you, Laine?"

I shake my pounding head.

"Look, Laine," she says, softening her voice. "I'm sorry about how I was the last time I saw you, OK? I've been pretty fucked up lately. You know. Just dealing with shit."

I automatically look at her wrists. "Are you OK?"

She shrugs. "You're still coming to the parties, huh?"

"Yup."

"So where are your friends this time?"

So much for sincerity.

"Inside," I say. "I just needed some fresh air."

"Uh-huh." She smirks like she knows I'm lying.

"I better go back inside," I say. "They're probably wondering where I am."

"Oh, Laine. Come on. You don't have to be afraid of me anymore."

"I'm not afraid of you," I lie. "I just think I should get back."

And I don't want to play your games.

"I think you're afraid."

"Why do you always do this?" I ask. I don't know

why I bother. I should just step off the gazebo and disappear.

"Do what?" she asks innocently.

"Act this way. Like you're playing some game. Like you're out to get me." I pause as the familiar fear courses through me. My heart pounds so hard in my chest it hurts. But instead of running away, I take a deep breath. "Why do you hate me so much, Leah?"

"Me?" She pretends to look surprised. "I could ask you the same thing. It's written all over your face, Lainey. Why do *you* hate *me*?"

"I don't hate you," I say. When I look her in the eye, I realize I mean it. I really don't hate her. "I just don't understand you."

"Heh. Mr. Mitchell." She moves a little on the bench, as if she's suddenly uncomfortable. "He was wrong, you know. You *can* understand something and still hate it."

"Like what?"

She turns and looks out into the dark behind us. "Like Sam," she says quietly. "I understand him now. And I hate him more than ever."

Sam. It seems to always come back to him.

Don't leave me alone with Sam.

"Why do you hate him?" I ask. My words sit between

us. I can almost see them. We lock eyes. Any other time I would have looked away. But not now. Maybe it's the beer that's given me confidence. I don't know. I don't care.

"You really have to ask?"

"Maybe you should tell me," I say. "Maybe you should say it out loud."

"What, you're my therapist now?" This time she's the one who looks away. "That's cute."

"You always told me if the truth was out, I would feel better. Why should it be different for you?"

She bites her bottom lip.

"Just say it."

She turns back to face me. "He did to me what I did to you, OK? Only worse."

The fear drains out of me and leaves a feeling in its place that I don't recognize. I open my mouth to say something, anything, but no words come to me. What could I possibly say?

"Yeah. Ya know what? I don't feel better," she says. "You make a shitty shrink, Lainey."

"I'm sorry," I say quietly. But the words feel meaningless.

"What are you sorry for?"

"I don't know." It's the truth. I really don't know. But I am.

182

"Now it's your turn," she says, moving closer to me.

"What do you mean?"

"Now you tell *me* the truth."

"The truth about what?"

"About us, Lainey. Just say it." Her words echo mine, and I realize how awful they must have sounded. "I want you to say it out loud, Lainey. Admit you liked what we did."

"No." I feel my fear sweep back through me again. I pull my legs up onto the bench and hug my knees to my chest.

"You know what the crazy thing is?" She stands up and comes closer to me. Her arms are crossed as she looks down at me, disgusted.

I squeeze my knees closer to my chest.

"I did that shit to you to get rid of it." I can almost feel her hate on my face as she spits the words. "I hated it. But you *liked* it! You *wanted* it! That's sick." Her eyes are filled with tears, but she doesn't cry.

"You're wrong," I say quietly. "I didn't know what you were doing."

"Bullshit."

"You said we were practicing!" I wipe my own tears away from my eyes before they can run down my cheeks. "You lied! Oh, my God. You—"

I hear her words again. *He did to me what I did to you.*

"You're just like Sam," I say. "You're worse than Sam."

"What?"

"You're no better than Sam!" I yell the words in her face.

"How could you say that?" She looks like she wants to kill me.

"You knew what you were doing! You just said you were getting rid of what he did to you by doing it to me. How sick does that make *you*, Leah?"

I feel the anger swelling up so fast I want to scream. All those years of her making me feel like I was the one who should be ashamed.

"Don't get all holy on me, Lainey. Don't you dare turn this back on me. You're no saint."

"What's that supposed to mean?" I ask. I'm holding my hands in fists so tightly, my fingernails dig into my palms.

"It means you could have done more," Leah says. "That day at the beach with Paige, you were so hell-bent to save her. But what about me? You never wanted to fucking help *me*!"

A tear slips down her own cheek before she turns away from me. "That's pretty sick, Laine," she says without turning back. "Don't you think?"

184

All at once my stomach convulses, and I run to the edge of the gazebo and throw up over the side.

When I finish, I turn back to face her.

"Why me?" I ask her. I give up on wiping my eyes. I don't care anymore if she sees me cry. "Why did you choose me?"

"Why *me*?" she says back. "Why Brooke?" She looks away again and dries her eyes with the palms of her hands.

"Why didn't you tell me?" I say. "I could have helped you. I would have helped you! We could have stopped him! Instead you—you tortured me with it."

She shakes her head.

"Why didn't you tell me?!"

She looks at me carefully, and I force myself not to look away.

"I would have helped you," I say. "You know that."

But she just shakes her head again. "I'm out of here."

"No," I say. "Answer me!"

"You don't want to know, Lainey. Trust me."

"Yes, I do."

"Then figure it out."

"How?!"

"Why didn't *you* stop me?" she asks quietly. Her tears are gone now. She looks like she wants to kill me, she hates me so much. "The truth, Lainey. You tell me the truth. You liked it. That's why. We both fucking liked it. We hated it, and we still wanted it. If you can't say the words out loud, I'll say them for you."

But before I can say anything, she steps into the dark and disappears.

LESSON 21

The truth will set you free.

The gazebo is quiet. I slide myself onto the cold, wooden floor and curl back into a ball.

You liked it. We both fucking liked it.

I squeeze my eyes closed and try to shut out her words by concentrating on the party noises in the distance. They sound like the hum of a TV when you're not watching.

The hard floor makes my head ache more than it did before, but I don't get up. I don't move. I feel all the ugliness and shame I've bottled up pour over me and cover me like a blanket.

Leah used me. She picked me because somehow she knew I would keep her secrets. Somehow she knew I would do whatever she wanted. She knew I wouldn't stop her. Somehow she knew. . . . She knew part of me would like it.

"Laine? Is that you?"

Web's warm hand presses against my shoulder and shakes me. I don't move. I don't want him to see me.

"Lainey? Jesus, are you OK?"

I cover my face with my hands.

"What's going on?" Jess comes around the other side and pulls my hands away.

"What's wrong, sweetie?"

I'm crying again. I sit up and look at them. Their innocent faces. How can I tell them the truth?

I wipe my face with my shirt. "Just drank too much," I say, trying to smile.

Web makes a face like he doesn't believe me. "Why are you crying?"

I shrug. "I have no idea!" I force a laugh. "Guess I just got kind of emotional about our last party."

Jess sits down next to me. "I saw Leah come in the back door, Lainey. Was she hassling you again?"

My hands are shaking. I pull my knees back to my chest and hug them to keep myself still. "Nah," I say, careful not to meet their eyes.

"Web, I peed in your mother's flowers," I say, trying to change the subject.

"Cool." He smiles that way he does, then puts his hand on my knee. "You sure you're OK?"

Tell him the truth, I think. *Just tell him.* I open my mouth. I don't know where I'll start, but if I can just say something, anything—

There's a shriek from inside the house and then a bunch of cheers.

"Shit, this is a crazy party," Web says, forgetting his question.

"Good thing it's the last one." Jess leans her head against mine.

"Let's go back in," Web says. "It's too cold out here." He holds his hands out to us and pulls us up.

"I hope you saved your bed for us, 'cause I need to pass out," Jess says.

Web takes his key chain out of his pocket and jingles it. "Kept it locked up just for you, my friends."

We each take his arm and let him lead us back toward the house. I feel the gazebo and the secrets it holds getting smaller behind me. I want to be happy. To finally just let the past slip away into the night. I pause and breathe in the cold, fresh air.

Web tugs my arm. "Come *on,* girlie! The night's still young!"

I fake a giggle and let him lead me back in.

The light in the living room is painfully bright. A bunch of people, including Lucas, are hanging out on the couch, passing around another joint. I think some of them are Jess's friends from Maine.

"Who's next?" asks a girl I don't know.

"Me," a voice says from behind us.

I spin around and look for the face that goes with it. She winks at me as if the conversation in the gazebo never took place, then walks past and reaches for the joint. Her eyes are slightly bloodshot, but no one would know it's because she's been crying. She takes a long, slow hit without taking her eyes off me. A hulky guy who looks like he's in his twenties steps up behind her and puts his hand around her waist. She breathes out and passes the joint to him. He makes a big production out of inhaling forever, then gives it to the person on the other end of the couch.

Web and Jess stand on either side of me, watching the joint get smaller as it makes its way along the couch. The whole time I feel Leah watching me, but I don't acknowledge her. When the joint reaches the far end of the couch again, the girl holds it out to Jess. She takes a quick hit and offers it to me, but I pass.

"I'll take it," Leah says. She licks her lips before bringing the joint to her mouth, then takes another long drag. As she breathes out, she makes a kiss with her lips and blows the smoke in my face.

"Come on, Lainey," she says, holding it out to me. "This is one thing we've never done together."

Her boyfriend half laughs, like he knows.

When she hands me the joint, she tickles the inside of my hand with her middle finger and winks at me. I pull my hand away fast.

I try to take a quick hit, but as soon as I bring the tip to my mouth, I feel her spit on my lips. I pass it to Web.

"Remember what good friends we used to be, Lainey?" Leah says, stepping closer to me. "We were really good friends. Friends forever. Remember?"

I take a step back. Everyone is looking at us.

Web moves closer to me, protectively. I don't know how he knows she's about to pounce.

"Ready to tell the truth yet, Laine?" she whispers, moving in even closer.

The truth. I don't even understand what the truth is anymore.

191

Her boyfriend takes her arm and gives it a tug. She flinches slightly, but recovers fast.

"I wish we were still special friends," she says louder.

I quickly glance over at the group on the couch again. Lucas is staring at me, totally intrigued.

"Leah, please," I say. "You're wasted."

"I am?" she says in mock surprise. Her boyfriend laughs uncomfortably and tugs her arm again.

"What do you want?" Jess asks, moving in close on my other side. She takes my hand protectively.

Leah notices our hands and laughs. "How interesting," she says. "You like that, Lainey?"

"Shut up," I say, letting go of Jess's hand.

"What's she talking about?" Jess asks. She steps back and takes Web's hand with the one that held mine.

"Nothing," I say.

"Oh, come on, Laine. Tell her. If you don't, I will."

"There's nothing to tell," I say. "You know that."

"Do I? Think about it, Laine. It's all still true. You *liked* it."

"No," I say. "I didn't understand."

"I think you did," she says, stepping closer. "Remember what you said to me earlier? 'Say it out loud. It will make you feel better.' Or does she already know your secret? Is she the one you practice with now?"

"What's she talking about?" Jess asks.

"Nothing," I say.

"Laine and I used to be special friends, didn't we, Laine?"

"Babe, come on," hulky boyfriend says, taking ahold of her arm. Leah smiles uncomfortably, like his grip is hurting her. I hope maybe that will be enough to stop her, but she seems to be on a maniacal roll.

"Leave me alone," she says to him. "Laine and I are talking."

"Why are you doing this?" I ask. I feel like a child. The corners of my mouth start to press down, the way babies' do before they start bawling.

"We used to kiss in Laine's special closet. Remember, Lainey?" she blurts out. She glances at the boyfriend quickly to check his reaction. His mouth drops open. I can't tell if he's shocked or turned on.

"No," I say.

"We did other stuff, too. Remember?"

"Shut up."

"Till we got caught."

Someone on the couch kind of laughs.

Web and Jess stand there, not saying anything. The room is totally silent. Web has this look on his face as if I've betrayed him. Like he believes her and not me, and that means I'm gay and I never told him. I'm sure Jess is totally freaked out. Maybe she's remembering our weekend in Maine and how she undressed in front of me. I feel the weight of their disappointment press on my heart. *Please*, I want to say. *Please*. But I don't even know what to ask for.

"We took turns, remember? First I did something to you, then you had to do it to me."

"No."

Tears slide down my cheeks, but I don't wipe them off. Leah reaches forward to touch my face. I slap it away.

She keeps talking, but I don't listen. I don't let myself hear her tell Web and Jess and her boyfriend and Lucas and a couch of strangers about all the things we did. As if they are things any two best friends would do. I just stare at her awful, beautiful face and hate her.

Finally, the boyfriend shuts her up.

"We're leaving." He wraps his pawlike hand around her arm and pulls her to him. He doesn't look happy.

Leah smiles at me pitifully. "See? That wasn't so bad, was it? It's good to get it out in the open. You've got to embrace your past, Lainey. That's the only way to get beyond it. You know I'm right. Right, Lainey? The truth will set you free and all that bullshit? I know *I* feel a hell of a lot better. Do you?"

But you didn't tell the whole truth, I think. *You didn't tell all of it.* Only her boyfriend is half dragging her away, and I don't have time to say the words.

Leah's heels click on the tile in the hallway. "You're hurting me!" her voice echoes back to us.

Jess and Web are behind me. I don't dare turn around. I wait for a second for one of them, either one, to put a hand on my shoulder, to tell me it's OK. But no one touches me. No one says a word before I take off down the hall after Leah.

LESSON 22

Be careful what you wish for.

Outside, Leah and her boyfriend are arguing by a car. He's still holding her arm.

Hurt her. She deserves it.

Leah says something I can't hear, and the guy stomps off, all pissed.

"Leah!" I yell.

She doesn't turn around.

I run toward her.

"Leah, wait!"

I'm sure she can hear me. But she doesn't turn around. She gets into a sports car parked a few cars over from my dad's truck and takes off down Web's long driveway.

"Fucking bitch!" the boyfriend yells. He heads off down the driveway after her, as if he could actually catch up.

I get into the truck, fumble for my keys, and turn the ignition. I pull out of the driveway, past the boyfriend waiting at the corner, and follow Leah. I'll follow her all the way home if I have to. I don't know what I'll say to her, but I have to confront her. I see the look of hate in her eyes again. Feel it grab hold of my heart. *Why does she hate me so much? Why did she do it? What's the real reason she chose me?* I have to know.

It's dark on the road. Bugs fly at the headlights. I know that as I drive, I'm killing them by the hundreds. I can almost feel them hitting the hood of the truck, the windshield. I want to stop. Just stop and not go any farther. But I see Leah's taillights way ahead, so I speed up to catch her.

Her brake lights go on in the distance, but as I get closer, she takes off again. I beep my horn, which is ridiculous, but I don't know what else to do.

I press the gas. The speedometer climbs from forty to fifty to sixty. I don't know the road well, but it's not a highway and there are some sharp turns. Up ahead there's a yellow diamond-shaped sign with a black squiggly arrow and a "REDUCE SPEED TO 25" warning.

Leah's brake lights go on, and I get close enough to see her license plate. I flash my lights at her and beep the horn again. She speeds up, crossing the double yellow lines.

The lines blur together through my tears. I blink, but it doesn't help. *Please stop. Please stop.* I only say the words in my head, but they choke me just the same. I don't want to think about how drunk and stoned she is, driving so fast. *Please stop.*

Finally she gets back on the right side, and I find my voice. "Pull over!" I yell to the back of her car. "Pull over before you get yourself killed!"

But as soon as the road straightens out, she goes even faster. My speedometer reaches seventy when I see another yellow sign with a curved black arrow. I wait for Leah's brake lights to come on, but nothing happens.

"Stop!" I yell at the windshield. "I'm not letting you get away, so just stop!"

But instead of braking, she goes faster. When she reaches the turn, I don't see her brake lights.

I quickly slam on my own brakes as I reach the turn. The truck's tires scream. The back end of the truck forces to the right, then the left.

I think I see yellow lights through the trees ahead,

but I don't realize until I stop and the lights are gone that they weren't mine. They were Leah's.

Where did she go?

The headlights of the truck light up the road and the trees on the other side of it. Finally I see a set of red taillights. But they aren't on the road. They're down the embankment, at the edge of the woods.

I open my door carefully. As soon as I do, the chime goes off, interrupting the silence around me.

Ding ding ding ding . . .

I step down and feel the hard pavement under my feet. I hold myself up with the door handle. My hand is shaking.

I slowly let go of the handle and cross the road to where I saw the taillights. I step toward the edge of the embankment, afraid to look. Below me, at the tree line, the black sports car is crumpled around a tree in a grotesque sort of hug.

I smell gas.

Everything is quiet except for the *ding ding ding* from the truck in the distance.

I climb carefully down the embankment.

The dew on the grass is cold and wet in my sandals.

The dinging is a whisper, calling me back to the road. But I keep moving toward the car.

The windshield is cracked into a spiderweb where her head hit but didn't go through.

I move closer.

It's still quiet. But now the crickets are beginning to join the steady dinging in the distance. And now the frogs.

The car is just out of reach of the truck's headlights. I pause, afraid to move into the darkness. The car's red taillights, like devil eyes, warn me away.

The smell of gas gets stronger as I force myself to move closer.

The driver's door is smashed inward.

The window is shattered.

I move closer, closer, listening for a sound from inside.

She's slumped over the steering wheel, not moving. But I see her pink halter. Her long, slender arms. Her blond, bloody hair.

I listen for a sound. A moan. Anything. But it is deadly quiet. So quiet. Except for the normal night sounds.

"Leah?"

She doesn't move.

"Oh, God. Leah!"

I start to reach inside to shake her, but I stop. Somehow I know.

I know.

"No," I say to her hair. "No!"

She doesn't move.

"Wake up!" I scream, even though I know she won't.

I hear the faint sound of sirens in the distance and panic. I turn and run back to the truck. Lights have come on in houses down the road. I get in and shut the door. The dinging stops, but my ears are ringing with the screaming in my head. *No! No! No!*

I put the truck in gear and drive, not knowing where to go.

The first thing I see when I open my eyes is the glove compartment of my father's work truck, held together with a twisted piece of coat hanger. My face feels stuck to the faded and dingy vinyl seat. Above me, the windows are all fogged up. Good. No one can see in. See me.

I breathe in the smell of my father's work: wood stain, old furniture, sweat. A faded green air freshener in the shape of a pine tree dangles uselessly from the rearview mirror.

I force myself to lift my head to see the clock on the

dashboard: 5:32 a.m. When I sit up, I feel the blood rush to my head. Everything hurts.

The key is still in the ignition. When I turn it, the motor starts reluctantly. I turn on the wipers to clear the dew on the windshield and immediately see the store window of the 7-Eleven. There are people inside buying coffee and scratch tickets and doughnuts. I put the truck in reverse before they notice me.

I drive home with the steady hum of the motor drumming into my head.

Leah's dead. Leah's dead. Leah's dead.

When I get home, I open the front door carefully. The house is quiet. I go upstairs, shut my bedroom door, and change into my pajamas. I shove all my dirty clothes under the bed, then crawl into it and listen to the quiet. Listen and think. Listen and try to feel something. Anything. But all there is, is numbness. Nothing. I am empty. I close my eyes and wait for my mother or the police or both to come and tell me what I already know.

Leah Greene is dead.

And it's my fault.

LESSON 23

When you break something,
fix it.

It's dark out. I don't know what time it is. It doesn't matter. All day I've been in and out of sleep, remembering. Ignoring my mother each time she climbs the stairs and asks if she can get me something.

I sit up and see myself in the mirror. I look dirty and matted and disgusting, as if I haven't showered in days.

I get up slowly, quietly, and creep to the bathroom. I turn the water on full and step in without waiting for the hot to kick in. The tub is cold against my skin. I reach for the soap and a washcloth and rub myself all over. Hard. I scrub and scrub until the water warms up and rises over my ankles, my shins, my knees. I scrub until my skin feels raw and the water is so hot it stings against my skin.

Leah Greene is dead.

It's all my fault.

Leah Greene is dead.

I lean against the hard back of the tub and close my eyes.

I see flashes of Leah. Hear fragments of her voice.

Remember, Lainey?

Remember when we used to mess around?

First I did something to you, then you had to do it to me. You liked it. You know you did.

Tears slip down my cheeks and along my neck. I sink under the water to wash them away. Under here, the quiet echo of the water moving makes me feel like I'm in another world. Alone. But I have to come up for air.

"Laine?" My mother knocks on the bathroom door. "Honey? What are you doing in there? Do you know how late it is?"

I don't know how late it is. I have no idea what time it is.

"No," I say from my side of the door.

"Honey, it's nine thirty. Can I — can I come in?"

I sit up. The cold air feels twice as bad after being underwater.

"I'm OK, Mom. I'll get out in a minute."

"Laine," she says softly. "I'm so sorry this happened. Don't you think—don't you think we should talk about it?"

Talk about what?

What does she know?

I don't even know what *I* know anymore. What was real? What did I imagine?

"Laine?"

"I'm OK, Mom. I just need to be alone. Just a little longer. Please."

I picture her on the other side of the door, leaning her head against the wood, wondering what she should do. "All right, honey. We'll talk later."

Later.

What happens next? Will the police come? Will they take me away?

I sink back down under the water again and listen to the water swish around me, wishing it would swallow me whole.

On the far wall is the door to the doll closet with the worn brass handle that Leah and I touched so many times. I know the nesting doll is in there, all broken on the floor.

Not long after Leah and I became friends, I made

the mistake of telling her that when I was really little, I used to think that my dolls and stuffed animals came alive when I left the room. She teased me, saying I still believed. She grabbed my old Curious George and punched him in the face. I laughed, just so she'd stop. But inside, I was cringing. After that, even though I was way too old to believe such a thing, I still imagined that the dolls who watched us in the closet hated Leah. I imagined them giving her the evil eye when we weren't looking.

I stand up in the tub and let the cold air rush over me. After I dry off, I put my robe on and tie it tightly across my waist. Then I reach for the handle to the closet and open the door.

As soon as I smell the room, old feelings rush through me. I hear her voice, feel her hand.

I can't do it.

How can I do it?

Slowly I force one bare foot forward across the cold wood floor. Then the other. I breathe in deeply before reaching my head in and pulling the tiny chain that clicks the lightbulb on.

It's the same as we left it. The little chairs and table are still there. The dolls sit neatly in the corner, still watching. Except for a few bags of outgrown clothes piled in the middle of the room, it looks exactly the same. And on the floor, there's the nesting doll, all in pieces.

Finally, I can't hold my breath anymore and let it out. When I breathe in again, I smell the dust and must and memories.

The little doll halves look up at me with their permanent, knowing smiles.

Slowly, I bend down and pick up the pieces. First the smallest one, then the next smallest. I fit them each inside the other until I close the last shell. I push the two pieces together snugly and glance over at the tiny space where it all started just one more time, before I click off the light.

Back in my room, I put the doll on my dresser, then find my warmest pajamas, grab my ratty old Curious George off the bookcase, and get into bed. Jack snuggles up next to me. I rest my face on his back, and he starts to purr. Soon his fur is wet with my tears. He pulls away, then comes back to sniff around my face. I make room for him next to me. I lean my face against his back again and listen to his deep, soft motor.

The doll stares at me from the dresser, smiling despite it all. I close my eyes, but I still feel her watching me. I can't take it.

I squeeze the doll in my hands as I carefully open my bedroom door. The house is quiet. I walk silently down the hall, through the darkened dining room, the kitchen, and to the back door. I slip on my mother's garden clogs, grab the flashlight by the hook next to the door, and step out into the dark.

The grass looks gray-green in the moonlight. I wait until I reach the edge of the woods and the short pathway that leads to the big rock before I turn on the flashlight. I walk the path quickly, still clutching the cold, hard doll in my hands. I feel the trees watching me, their branches ready to reach out and grab me. I want to turn and run back to the house. But I don't. I get to the rock and kneel down next to it. I place the doll beside the flashlight in the dried leaves. The ground is soft there, and I dig up the leaves and dirt with my hands until I have a hole big enough to bury the doll. I place her in face up, then quickly cover her with the dirt and leaves. I shine the flashlight on the spot. It looks the same way it did before. No one will find her here.

I turn off the light as soon as I reach the backyard safely. Then I quietly make my way back to my room and climb into bed next to Jack and George.

Tomorrow, I think to both of them. *Tomorrow I will tell the truth.*

I fall asleep to images of Leah. We're twelve again, cantering around the riding ring, doing our victory lap. Leah waves the strip of newspaper in the air as she turns back to me. "We did it!" she yells over and over again. I wave my own empty hand in the air, following behind her, smiling so hard my face hurts as the crowd cheers, and I make a secret wish that this moment will last forever. That we'll just keep riding around and around, laughing and waving to each other.

But I wake up alone in my dark room instead. And when I close my eyes again, I dream that she's riding away from me. And instead of waving the strip of paper over her head like before, she's looking back at me, waving her empty hand. Waving good-bye.

LESSON 24

The truth belongs to you.

What happens when you finally decide to tell the truth and no one listens?

Three weeks have passed since Leah died. The Greenes held a private service for family only and buried Leah in a tiny cemetery near their home. Leah and I used to ride our bikes here and dare each other to go inside the gate, though we never did it.

It seems strange to me now, as I sit here under a wide oak tree in front of Leah's grave, that we were ever afraid of this peaceful place.

I tried to tell the truth about what happened that night. First to my parents, then to the police. But they all said it was clear from the lack of skid marks on the road and the alcohol and drug content in Leah's blood what really happened.

What really happened?

Leah was drunk. Leah was stoned. Leah was going too fast.

She didn't even try to take the turn.

She went straight off the road.

"But it was *me*," I told them. "She was going too fast because of *me*. I was the reason—"

"It doesn't matter," the police officer told me. "You weren't doing anything wrong. That girl had a death wish. Just look. Look at the evidence."

He told me about the scars on her wrist that I never saw. He reminded me about the drugs in her system. He told me, quietly, about the bruises they found on her ribs, back, and upper thighs that had been on her body before the accident.

"That girl had some serious problems," he said. "She was headed for disaster."

"But I left," I tried. "I left her there."

He nodded and was quiet for a minute. "Your friend died the second she hit that tree. You couldn't have saved her. Losing your friend? That's gonna stay with you the rest of your life. Whatever you think you did, that's up to you to figure out."

I'm still trying.

If what he said is true, and Leah really did have a death wish, I believe I was in the very place Leah wanted me to be. I think she wanted me to see her drive away from me.

I've rethought a thousand times the way she looked at me that night. I was so sure it was hatred toward me. But now I think maybe it was the hate she felt for herself. I think she hated herself for what she let happen to her as much as I hated myself for what I let happen to me. We were both victims. I know that now.

I went back there, to the place it happened, a few days after the accident. There were stuffed animals and candles and letters for Leah all over the side of the road where the tire tracks led into the woods.

I don't think it was the memorial Leah would have liked. I think she would have preferred a more dramatic funeral, like the ones on her mom's soap operas. Sam would have been there, looking guilty. Maybe he would have stood dramatically and confessed to what he'd done to damage her all those years ago. And the boyfriend. He would have stood, too, and wept like a baby and said how sorry he was for hurting her. Maybe all the boys who used her would show up, crying and remorseful.

Brooke would be there, too, and Christi. They'd be properly sad and big-sisterish. And our parents would be sobbing down in the front row.

And where would I be, that plain, quiet girl Leah was always dragging along?

I'd be up at the front, where everyone could see me.

I would stand at the altar above Leah's shiny coffin and deliver the eulogy. I would tell the truth about Leah Greene. I would say she was my troubled friend. I would admit that I let her down. I would explain that, in many ways, we let each other down. But I would say that I forgive her. And while I spoke, I'd feel her watching and listening, trying to decide if she forgives me, too.

Instead there was only a sad roadside altar of cheap stuffed animals and plastic flowers put there by people who didn't really know Leah at all.

It's different here, though. It's only me. Jess and Web drive me here, but they wait in the parking lot. I know they don't understand why I come here, but they are my friends, so they don't ask why.

They never did. They just showed up after it happened, sat on my bed with me, and let me tell them the truth. All of it.

When I finished, Web looked at me and shook his head.

"That girl really messed you up," he said.

Jess put her hand on mine. "But you have us now."

"Yeah," Web said. "And we'll only mess you up in a good way!"

Jess elbowed Web, and then they both hugged me. I let them fold me into their warm arms before I pulled back.

"Thank you," I said.

"We didn't do anything," Web said.

But they had. They passed the friendship test.

Now I sit and look at Leah's name, perfectly and permanently etched into the polished black granite stone. When I move, I can make out the reflection of my shape, and I imagine it's Leah looking back at me.

I don't speak out loud. I don't want to interrupt the sounds around us. The birds singing to one another, the wind softly swimming through the leaves above us. Instead, I talk to her inside my head. I tell her I think I understand why she did what she did. That in some strange way, I'm grateful for all the painful lessons because of what they taught me in the end. I tell her that even though I still don't completely understand why she did all the things she did, I really do forgive her.

I tell her I'm sorry I didn't see all the trouble she was in. I tell her I'm sorry I didn't push her to tell me

214

about Sam sooner or try harder to find out if the suicide rumors were true. I tell her I did care, but I was so caught up in being hurt and scared and hating her, I didn't see her pain. And I ask her to forgive me back.

I nod to say good-bye, and I almost believe she's nodding back at me.

But she's not.

It's me nodding. Me nodding to her, and to myself. When I stand, I see the shape of my legs reflected in the stone. I step backward. Backward. Backward until I can't see my image there anymore. Then I turn and walk away.

In the distance, I see Web and Jess leaning against Web's car. When they see me coming, they wave, as if I wouldn't be able to find them in the nearly empty lot. I wave back, smiling for the first time I can remember. And then, instead of walking back to them, I start to run.

ACKNOWLEDGMENTS

Thank you to all the people who've read this story at various stages and encouraged me to keep going. Thank you to Lowry Pei and Angelique Davi, my very first readers. Thank you to Cecil Castellucci for her friendship, love, and unconditional faith; to Holly Black for the call that made everything click; and to Sarah Aronson, Darlene LaCroix, and Cynthia Lord for their honest and valuable feedback. Thanks to my WWaWWa sisters, Cindy Faughnan and Debbi Michiko Florence, who read multiple revisions and never once dropped their virtual pompoms. To my agent, Barry Goldblatt, for believing in me when I didn't, and to my editor, Joan Powers, who always started with the good stuff and asked all the right questions. Extra special thanks to my husband, Peter Carini, for everything. And finally, thank you to the PEN New England Children's Book Caucus for selecting *Lessons from a Dead Girl* as the winner of their 2005 Discovery Award. I am forever grateful.